A COUNTRY STRANGER

KIMBERLEY KELLER

CHAPTER 1

Torrential rain battered my sister's tiny, little car. Muddy water splashed up from a pothole in the road. The tall trees to either side of the country lane were my only saving grace from the strong winds. I got momentarily stuck between gears, revving the engine ridiculously as I panicked.

She hadn't agreed to let me borrow her car. She knew nothing about it. I'd taken it while she was on a business trip to Moscow. It was her little, pink pride and joy and I was wrecking it.

To make matters worse, I was completely lost and my mobile phone was dead.

Lightning struck.

I held my breath.

It was forked lightning. And I saw it land somewhere over the horizon of the hill ahead.

Thunder rolled almost immediately.

The storm was only getting heavier, my wipers were at maximum and still the rain obscured my vision.

I tried the radio again. There was no signal.

The moon was somewhere up there, behind all those vast, ugly clouds.

I eased the little car carefully onwards, fearful one of these potholes would be deeper than the last and I'd do permanent damage to her vehicle.

Max, you spoilt brat, I could already hear her say, *how dare you take my car without asking!*

And she'd be right.

I should've been at home, studying for my University exams next month, not out cruising the countryside in search of some random person I'd swiped right for. It'd obviously been a joke. They were out of my league. And I should've known better.

I stopped the car.

There was a series of thunderclaps, but I'd missed the lightning.

I needed to get back to the motorway. If I could find my way out of this dense, forest maze and back to a main road, I was sure I could figure my way home even without a working smartphone.

I couldn't make my mind up whether to drive on or to turn back.

I'd already been driving for several miles, and I'd taken a dozen turns from one lane to the next. Half of those had been when following my GPS for directions to my not-so-booty call, the other half had been me trying to correct myself to no avail.

I decided to throw the car around, initiating a three-point turn. The road was extremely narrow though, with walls of rock to either side, so I had to be careful. This'd be a seven-point turn at least-

BANG!

"Shit!" I looked over my shoulder.

The red brake light was shining right up against the rocky wall. I'd reversed Jenny's car straight into it!

Rain pelted the roof even heavier.

I pulled my denim jacket tight to my chest, then shoved the door open and stepped out.

Huge gusts of wind pushed me back as I struggled along the side of the car towards the rear. The rain was so strong it hurt as it struck the soft skin of my face.

"Oh no," I said aloud, my heart sinking as I saw one of the brake lights shattered.

I armed rain from my brow, then crouched in the muck to inspect for further damage. Moisture seeped through my jeans as I checked, immediately superseding the damage as chief among my concerns. Well, they were a new pair after all!

But Jenny was still going to kill me. The wall had scraped the paintwork.

This would require serious cash to repair.

And I didn't even have enough to fill up the tank for her as a thank you.

I gripped the car for support, and pulled myself back to my feet-

My fingers slipped on the wet metal, the soles of my shoes slid on the muddy grass, and I fell flat on my ass.

I was winded, and lay still for several seconds.

The radio suddenly picked up a signal and started playing Snow Patrol's Chasing Cars. The irony of lying here was not lost on me.

Lightning flashed overhead, forking into the trees just behind me.

I rolled onto my side, saturating myself in yet more mud.

I put my filthy palms down, and pushed myself up, then

staggered to the car. I realised I'd taken quite a bump on the way down.

I slid onto the driver's seat, dirtying Jenny's custom-made expensive seat, and turned down the radio as the signal went static again.

I turned the key in the ignition, then gently lay my foot on the accelerator.

The car stayed stationary, although the engine was definitely working.

I applied more pressure.

Still, the car wouldn't move.

I looked in my near wing mirror, and saw the rear wheel chucking up mud against the wall.

"No, no, no," I cried, realising the car was stuck. How'd that happened so quickly?

More water flowed down from the horizon of the hill. Dirty water. The entire rear of the vehicle was becoming submerged in wet soil. All the front tyres did was point in a direction. There was no power in them.

I stamped on the accelerator regardless!

It was useless.

I opened the driver's side door and looked under the car. Water was flowing at an increasing rate. If I didn't free the car now, it'd be caught up and swept away as the road flooded.

I dropped my foot into the water, found the road beneath the surface, and tried to use it for leverage to haul the car out of the ditch.

Rain pelted the windscreen. Wind blew water into the car. More lightning forked overhead.

I reluctantly got out, and shielded my face from the elements as I went back to the rear. I grabbed hold of the bumper, and tried to pull with all my minimum might.

Thunder snarled.

I grimaced as I tried everything I could to free the vehicle, but with no one around to help it was useless.

I looked up the hill. Yet more flood water was flowing and the rain was only coming down harder.

Jenny was going to kill me!

Lightning struck above, sending sparks into the air.

I twirled around to see it'd hit a tree and the leaves were all lit up from the impact-
As a heavy branch crushed me underneath.

<u>CHAPTER 2</u>

I could hear a high-pitched ringing in my ear, which swiftly subsided when I realised there was water rushing over me.

I was still on the road, lying under the branch.

Had I been unconscious? If so, for how long?

My body was wet and cold all over.

I tried to move-

The branch had me pinned down.

I pushed at it, but it wouldn't budge.

More water flowed over my legs and my crotch, soaking me right through.

I tried harder at the heavy branch, which covered me from arm to arm and stretched across my chest. My heart pumped faster, as panic began to set in. What if I really couldn't move it?

I looked again at the water flowing down from the hill, then I glanced to the car. What if the water pushed the car on top of me?

I desperately attempted to wriggle free.

More water splashed up on my torso.

I hoped it could help dislodge the branch.

Branch!?! It was more like an entire tree trunk on top of me!

Jenny's car creaked next to me!

I didn't like that sound. Not at all. Could I really lose my life so simply, and all because I was chasing a bit of sex on a bloody dating app?

I grunted as I forced my fingers into the bark of the branch, grimacing and almost growling with the more effort I made.

My face was pelted with ever more rain.

A strong gust blew against the car.

I let out a long, frustrated exhalation as I took a momentary breather. I didn't know what I'd be able to do, but I couldn't give up. I just couldn't.

As the rain only got heavier and more floodwater rushed down from the top of the hill, my fears amplified. I really could die out here!

The water level rose above my stomach.

I could feel it, cold and unforgiving, rush into my ears.

"Help!" I cried out.

I pushed and struggled at the branch, kicking my legs out from the water too.

The storm pummelled mercilessly on, as yet more lightning struck somewhere behind the trees.

I was terrified, realising there was nothing I could do and there wasn't anyone around to save me.

"Help me somebody!" I squealed.

Thunder roared, as if damning me to hell for taking Jenny's car.

Water splashed up on my face.

I'd be under it in no time.

I sucked for air while I still could.

Water lapped at the log.

"Anybody? Please he-"

Water splashed up on my face and landed in my mouth.

I coughed it up.

Jenny's face flashed across my mind. She wasn't angry. She wasn't happy. She was sad.

I was really going to-

"HELP ME!"

die.

I had to slam my lips shut and arch my neck to my force my nostrils above the surface of the water. It was the only way I could breathe.

I couldn't even call for help again.

My body was almost entirely submerged.

I frantically kicked my legs for a few seconds, then stopped to conserve energy.

My eyes were under the water.

This was the most hellacious manner in which I could've imagined dying.

I thought I heard Jenny's car move.

The sound of everything was so distorted under the water.

If I didn't drown I'd be crushed.

Water started to slip into my nostrils.

I tried to dislodge the branch.

Lightning lit up the water above me.

I felt I was going to choke.

I wanted to struggle.

I somehow started to relax.
The lightning stayed on.
The lightning what?
That wasn't possible.
I turned my head, and the water rushed right up my nostrils.
But there was... Light?
There was...
I faded...
Out.

CHAPTER 3

I gasped. There was air. Lots of air. I could breathe!

I put my palm on my naked chest. My heart was beating. And normally.

My *naked* chest?

I was under a duvet, but *where* the hell was I? I didn't know this barely-lit room, did I?

I rubbed my eyes, then looked again. I certainly did not know this room.

I scented the remnants of the rain water still in my nostrils.

I ran my hand lower and found I wasn't wearing any clothes at all. Who'd saved me? And then undressed me? And what did they make of how I'd removed all my body hair except for a little landing strip above my crotch when I thought I'd set myself up for a naughty online date?

I could still hear the storm outside, battering the walls of wherever I was.

I pulled back the duvet, then started to move, creaking the springs of the old bed. I paused, my head sore and my chest aching from where the branch had fallen on it.

"You're awake," said a male voice, matter-of-factly.

I shot my eyes to the doorway, and saw him for the first time. I immediately covered my crotch with the duvet.

He seemed unfazed, his face lit by the hall light. "How do you feel, you okay?"

I was distracted by his physical appearance. He was rugged, but I liked that. A country guy, but I liked that too. And downright manly, which was no contest.

"You hear me?" he demanded.

"Sorry," I said, sheepishly. "I'm confused. Where am I?"

He walked into the room, wearing a red and black checked lumberjack shirt and ripped jeans (not designer, ripped by hard graft). "I heard you screaming for help on the road."

Screaming? He made me sound like such a sissy. "Thank you so much-"

"By the pink car."

I gulped.

"I rescued you in my tractor."

My eyes lit up. "Your tractor? Did you save the car?"

He glared at me. "No."

"It's my sister's."

"It's miles away," he said, gruffly.

Miles away? How far had he taken me?

"Probably lost to the elements." He looked at my chest. "That was a heavy bark you had on top of you. You'd have died if I hadn't come along when I did."

I ran my hand through my long hair. "I know, I don't know where to start to thank you-"

"Chores," he said. "Plenty of 'em need done around here. That storm's bedded in for a while now. You can help out 'round the house while you wait it out."

I nodded. "Of course. I'm so grateful... Mr?"

"Grady."

I put out my hand. "Nice to meet you, Mr Grady-"

"It's just Grady." He shook it, then grinned. "You've very soft hands."

I'd been told that a hundred times before, but never had I felt so intimidated than in front of this masculine giant. "I'm Max."

He ran his tongue behind his top lip, then over his front teeth. "Max, okay. I had to strip you..."

Why had I been unconscious for that?

"Your clothes were soaked right through. Leaving you in them could've led to pneumonia, hypothermia or death."

I nodded, trying not to do so too profusely.

"How do you feel, Max?"

I felt dampness through my hair. "I think I'm okay, Grady."

"Try to stand," he insisted.

What? But I was naked.

"Go on." He put his hands out. "I've got you."

I was both frightened and slightly aroused at the thoughts of falling into this behemoth's arms. "Erm, who else lives here?"

"No-one. Now stand up, Max. I need to know if you're injured. The nearest hospital's too far to make it in this weather and I haven't got a phone."

No phone?

"My mother lives in the next cottage up."

Ah, she had a phone-

"She doesn't have a phone either. So we need to know if you're an emergency."

I felt reassured at the *we* comment. At least someone else knew I was here.

"Stand," he said firmly.

I'd been naked in front of a few men before, but never one so hands-dirty-handsome nor so straight.

"Jesus, Max." He yanked the duvet from my body. "I stripped you."

Surely a more polite word would've been undressed?

"I've seen you."

I didn't have time to worry about etiquette, and set my feet on the floor, then pushed myself up from the bed.

Grady nodded. "Balance okay?"

I lifted one foot, then swapped to stand on just the other. "Fine."

"Turn," he said.

What?

"See if you get dizzy."

I was relieved to turn my petite penis away from his view, and admittedly felt a thrill when my bare, smooth ass was before him.

He inhaled.

I fantasised that he'd noticed it, but I doubted this country guy even believed in marriage equality never mind that he could find my body attractive.

"Okay, Max, you seem fine."

I'd been called *fine* before.

"You should take a shower, get heat into your bones."

I held my palm over my crotch. "Thanks, Grady. This where you live?"

He looked at me like I'd just asked the stupidest question in the world. "Yes."

"No, sorry, I mean... Is it a house? A farm?"

"It's a cottage, Max," he said, his voice bordering between frustration and offence. "On a farm." He put his fingers on my lower back, and pushed me forward. "You'll find the bathroom out there in the hall."

I tried to walk without my usual effeminate manner, and even felt relief to get away from his eyes when I got into the hall. I saw my jeans and denim jacket on a radiator, then felt them. They were still soaking. I checked the radiator. It wasn't even on.

"I'll leave some clothes on the bed for you to wear," Grady called from the bedroom.

"Thanks," I said, already wondering how I'd fit into anything a man twice my size had to share.

CHAPTER 4

I heard Grady whistling outside the bathroom, as I showered in the most incredible, soothing hot water. I felt so many of the stresses my body had been put through wash away as I turned around, warming my rear.

It was so hard to believe I could've been killed earlier by this same substance. I'd *really* nearly died. If Grady hadn't heard my cries, I'd have died. Either from drowning under that bloody log or crushed by the car.

Shit. Jenny's car. Lost.

Gusts of wind shook the cottage.

I made a mental note to ask him to clarify what he'd said about her car being miles away. Miles? What was he doing so far from home in that storm? What if he asked me what I was doing? I didn't fancy telling this old school man I'd been cruising for casual sex.

He whistled again.

Just how close was he? It sounded like he was just out in the-

The bathroom door opened, and Grady walked in. "Just bringing you a towel, Max."

I froze.

"A fresh one."

"Er... Thanks."

He looked over the frosted part of the glass, right at me. "It'll cover your midriff. Do you need another for your hair?"

I shook my head.

"You sure?"

"I'm sure, Grady," I said, and made my eyes tell him I wanted him to leave.

He nodded, set the towel down on the tiled floor, then walked out. He left the bathroom door wide open.

I told myself to be grateful, he'd just saved my life, and tried to shrug off the inappropriate behaviour. Country fold could be eccentric. And, besides, I could've tried to lock the door if it'd been unwelcome.

Behave, my instincts told me. Grady was a strong, traditionally masculine man. He *had* to be heterosexual. And he'd probably kick

me half to death if my behaviour suggested anything else.

"Grady," I called out, wrapping the towel high enough to cover my nipples and stretching it low enough to cover my little penis, "you wouldn't happen to have a spare charger for a-"
"No," he said flatly.
I *hated* being cut off from the outside world.
"Mobiles are a waste of time out here... Never get a signal."
I wanted to know where we were, but I was still so wary of my host. I didn't want to reveal I'd been completely lost. I walked out of the bathroom, down the hall and into the bedroom.
Grady was stood in front of the bed with his arms folded. "And I know you're a city kid."
Kid? "I'm twenty-one, Grady."
He pointed to my crotch, then gave a laugh. "I meant the way your pubic hair's groomed."
I blushed.
"Men out here in the country'd never do that."
I swallowed.
"But maybe it's wrong of me to judge you as a man."
This was not a conversation I was comfortable having with him so soon, and I probably never would be. Besides, I planned on being away in the morning.
"None of my clothes would fit you, Max."
I unintentionally shrugged, and hoped it didn't come across as ignorant or ungrateful. I was just uncomfortable at his tone.
"Your clothes aren't going to be fit for wearing for a couple of days."
I *definitely* wouldn't be here in a couple of days.
"So I left you out these," Grady said, stepping to one side and gesturing to the bed.
I was already feigning an appreciative smile before I realised what was laid out for me.
"Oh, you like them? Good."
My heart was pumping.
"Great, in fact. I wasn't sure if you'd be offended."
My pulse thudding.
"They belonged to my cousin's daughter."
And blood was rushing to my sex.

"She's grown out of them."

My jaw had dropped.

"Say something, Max."

I was speechless.

"Come on," Grady insisted, and reached out to guide me forward to the bed. "It's okay. I've seen your pink car. I've seen your landing strip."

I looked at him. *He* knew what that was called?

"These really are the only items that'll fit you."

I took a closer glance. Oh my God, he'd left out underwear too! Little white panties and a matching bra!

"Shit, Max, I almost forgot." Grady dug his right hand into his jeans' pocket and produced a pair of white lace, frilly ankle socks. "Have to keep your feet warm after the fright you had in the storm, right?"

I stared in disbelief at the bed. There was a short grey pleated skirt and a white blouse set neatly out before me.

"Say something then."

I was clutching my stomach through my towel. "Grady... I... Don't know what to say."

"Thanks would at least be a start."

Thanks?

"I wouldn't let anyone wear her clothes, y'know."

I mistakenly found his eyes.

Grady gazed back, all domineering.

"I can't wear these," I said, even though the thoughts of wearing them for someone excited me no end.

His face changed.

"No, no, no, Grady, I meant no offence-"

"Yes, you did. I see who you are. You think you're better than me because you're from the big smoke."

I shook my head.

Grady pulled my towel away from my body. "If you don't like these clothes, if you don't *appreciate* my generosity at all, you can run about the house naked for all I care."

I hesitated, unsure of my next move. I'd nowhere else to go and nothing else to wear-

"Although I don't think mother would appreciate her only son having a naked temptress hanging around the cottage all day."

A temptress? All day?

Grady put his hand around my upper arm, easily closing his palm on my slender form. "Wear the clothes for me, okay?"

I reluctantly nodded.

He let go of me, then started to walk out of the bedroom. "Now, *Maxine...*"

Maxine?

"About those chores..."

CHAPTER 5

I was stood at the stove in the kitchen-cum-living room of Grady's cottage, dressed in a full schoolgirl uniform, and slaving over a meal for him in return for his hospitality.

Rain hammered on one window and wind smacked leaves of a nearby tree off another.

I was acutely aware of the front door in the middle of the room, but reasoned it was extremely unlikely anyone would call in the middle of a storm. And if his mother did surely he'd more face to lose than I?

I stirred the pot, as steam rose to the extractor fan, then glanced at Grady.

He was looking at my bare legs.

I couldn't make my mind up about him. Did I find him attractive? Yes, in an almost Neanderthal manner of speaking. Did I think he wanted to hurt me? I reckoned he wanted to humiliate me. But did I believe he was sexually attracted to me dressed as a girl? I was too afraid to commit to that suspicion.

I had to undo the top couple of buttons on my white blouse because of the heat.

Grady wolf-whistled at me.

I ignored him.

"Is it warm in the kitchen?" he called, laid out on the sofa with his newspaper.

"Yes," I said, meekly.

"It's kind of cold in here." Grady got up, then went to the fireplace. "And I don't want you catching cold on my watch. I already saved your life once."

I felt a sensation within my cotton white panties.

Grady started the old-fashioned coal fire in the living room. "Now *that's* a man's job," he said, and walked into the adjoining kitchen behind me.

I felt the back of his hand breeze against the rim of my skirt.

"You able to find everything you needed okay?"

"Yes, Grady."

He laughed. "You're a good girl. Traditional. You know where to find stuff. I like that."

I said nothing. His comments didn't offend me, nor did his tone. I just didn't know this guy. And having me dress up in this, admittedly sexy, schoolgirl costume set off alarm bells. Alarm bells which could've aroused me in a different setting. Such as after a hook-up in a gay bar.

There was a sound of metal scraping on concrete just outside.

"Wow," Grady said, looking out the window. "That's the patio table blowing in the storm. And I weighed that shit way down this afternoon."

All I could imagine was Jenny's little car, probably smashed into a hundred different pieces by now.

"You can kiss goodbye to your pink wheels, Maxine."

I looked at him. "How'd you know what I was thinking?"

Grady's eyes were on my blouse, in particular on my flesh at the top. "I forgot to find you a tie."

I sighed. "I don't want it."

He drank in my figure, from my size 8 waist to my hips, my thighs and finally my frilly sock-clad feet. "Hey, seriously though, are your feet not feeling the cold?"

I lifted them both in succession, then set them down again on the kitchen floor. "A little."

"Okay, wait there."

Like I was going anywhere. I stirred some more.

"Good ol' Grady's gonna take good care of you."

I watched him walk out to the hall, then listened to his footsteps lead him back to the bedroom. I couldn't even guess as to what he was up to now.

"Now, you don't have to wear these," he called back. "But I *do* want you to. I want you to stay healthy. And warm."

I armed perspiration from my brow.

"Let's see what you think."

I quickly reached under my pleated skirt and fixed my panties around my genitals, as unbecoming sweat pooled at my scrotum.

Grady walked back in, holding up an incredible pair of black stiletto heels.

My jaw dropped.

"What d'you think?" he asked.

I *loved* them! "They're alright." They were like fucking stripper heels!

"Can I put them on you?"

"You?" I stared at him, with one eyebrow raised.

Grady set them next to the stove. "Put them on yourself, then. I was only trying to be helpful."

I turned the dial to zero. "Dinner's about ready to be served."

He appeared to be in a strop.

I raised one of my feet all the way up to the edge of the counter next to the stove, revealing my long, smooth legs. "Care to help a girl?" I asked, surrendering my voice to femininity.

His face flushed red, and he smiled. "Absolutely." Grady grabbed one heel, and began to slip it onto my foot.

Oh my God, my instincts – no, my hopes – were right about him!

He swiftly fastened the straps.

"It fits perfectly, Grady."

He lowered my leg to the floor, then lifted the other, subtly stroking my skin for just a second. "I'll put the other one on you, then we can sit around the table, eat our dinner and have a chat. I'd really like to get to know you, Maxine."

I gazed back at him. What else could I say? I'd already committed. "I'd really like to get to know you too, Grady."

CHAPTER 6

The wind wailed like a banshee in some eerie, backward place in the middle-of-nowhere.

And I was dressed up as a slutty schoolgirl in front of a man several years older.

I set the table, as he watched me... As he *leered* at me.

"You do that very elegantly," he said.

I was blushing again.

"I'm so hungry, Maxine."

I began to serve him my speciality. "I hope you like this, Grady."

He rubbed his stomach through his checked shirt. "If it tastes as good as it smells, I certainly will... I love spaghetti bolognese."

I'd made plenty of it, much more than I'd ever contemplate making for myself or anyone I tended to socialise with. Then again, I guessed I worried more about my figure than a real man like Grady.

He gestured to the chair opposite him. "Sit down. I can take it from here." He threw what could be described as a shitload of salt on his food.

I groaned, sitting my skirted-ass on the seat. "I used plenty of salt in the preparation."

He kept tossing on more. "I can never get enough."

I watched in disbelief.

Grady noticed.

I started to eat. "It's a shame I couldn't find any garlic bread. It goes so well with-"

"No garlic bread. Not tonight. It'd stink our breath."

I crossed my legs. Why would our breath matter? There was a storm on. We weren't going anywhere.

"Mother wouldn't approve," Grady said.

I tried to pull my short skirt lower, and sincerely doubted any of these clothes came from his cousin's daughter. With the storm only appearing to worsen, I felt it best to play along.

"So, Max..."

I was Max again?

"Do you have a girlfriend?"

I giggled. "Definitely not."

Grady chewed his food for several seconds. "Boyfriend?"

I shook my head.

"Interesting," he said, nodding.

How was *that* interesting? I wanted to know, and yet I didn't want to know. Every time I started to relax around this guy I had to remind myself he was a total stranger, even though he'd saved my life. And a lot of his behaviour was extremely odd. For all I knew I was in a state of shock after nearly drowning. Perhaps my senses were completely skew-whiff.

Grady pointed to my chest with his knife. "I'm pleased to see you went with the bra, Maxine. Pokies might be acceptable in the city, but you're in the country now, girl."

The tree leaves again battered the window.

"You've no need to be quiet," he insisted. "I want you to talk."

I was finding it hard to eat. Butterflies were flying around my stomach. And I couldn't make my mind up if it was through fear or attraction. "You mentioned your mother, Grady. Is it just you and her or-"

"I'm an only child."

"I see... Just cousins then."

He eyed my blouse. "Yes, Maxine, just cousins... And nieces and nephews. I don't see them much, so it's just me to look after mother. I'm in and out of her cottage several times a day."

"That's sweet," just slipped out of me. "Wait, does she have a phone?"

"No."

I sighed.

"I told you that already."

And I still didn't believe him.

"What about your family, Maxine?"

"Dad took off when I was little. My mother died when I was eleven. It's just me and my sister Jenny. And it's been that way for a decade." I sucked in a long line of spaghetti. "She's away on business in Moscow for the week."

Grady smiled. "So, no one to worry about you now you've gone missing?"

My heart skipped a beat. "That was her car you found me by."

Grady laughed. "Oh, Maxine, don't play coy... That little, pink fuck machine... Surely it was yours?"

I almost lost my breath. "Grady!"

He giggled.

"It's hers," I insisted.

"Pity... It suited you... Especially how you're dressed now."

I was dying to ask him where the outfit had really come from. Did he like girls? Or did he like sissies like me who cross-dressed? "What age are you, Grady, if you don't mind me asking?"

"I'm forty-two."

Wow. Twice my age. That wasn't a problem. I'd slept with older.

"This really is good, girl," he said, downing a dollop of mince. "But what I'd really like to know is why were you out there in that storm in the first place... Maxine."

I was almost enjoying how my new name sounded on his tongue, in that sexy, masculine manner he drawled. "Oh, it doesn't matter. I was lost."

"I know you were lost, but how did you come to be lost? You must've been going somewhere."

I shook my head.

"Or meeting *someone*."

Jesus, he was pushy! "Grady, I-"

"Who was the landing strip for?"

"Can we change the subject please?"

He gulped down his food. "Who was the lucky guy?"

"Nobody," I insisted. "I didn't meet anyone."

"I found these in your denim jacket," Grady said, then tossed three condoms onto the table.

My face immediately reddened.

"You a giver or a taker, Maxine?"

Taker.

"With a name like that?"

Taker! A big taker!

"Let me guess..."

I cleared my throat. "This conversation is totally inappropriate, Grady."

He burped.

I put my knife and fork down. "Perhaps I should leave."

"Excuse me," he said, covering his mouth. "You're welcome to leave, sweet cheeks, but have you looked outside recently?"

The cottage was silent inside. Outside, wind screeched and rain smacked off the walls like rat-a-tat-tat reminders of how isolated and in his debt I was.

"I didn't think so, Maxine."

"What would your mother think?" I demanded. "Tell me, what would she have to say about this if she walked in right now and saw me dressed like this in your company?"

"Stop it," he said.

"No, what would your mother say if she saw me dressed up like a schoolgirl slut for you?"

Grady slid his chair back, and stood. "Don't talk about my mother!"

I froze.

"Ever!" He walked towards the front door and lifted a heavy coat. "I'm going up to check on her. Have that table tidied and the plates and cutlery washed for me coming back. Understand?"

I was sniffling. "Yes, Grady... I'm sorry." I half-turned towards him, leaving my legs just over an inch apart. I knew he'd be able to see the whites of my cotton panties.

He threw on his coat.

I watched him.

He stopped. Then looked at me. He came at me.

I flinched.

"Thank you for dinner, Maxine." He leaned his lips down to me.

I turned my face away.

He placed a peck on my cheek.

My little penis throbbed.

"I mean it, honey, thank you."

I looked at his plate, and saw he'd only eaten half.

Grady opened the front door, and the noises from outside were horrendous, animals seemingly going ballistic and the thunder even louder than the rainfall.

"Grady!" I shouted.

"Yes?"

I hesitated, then crossed my legs. "Be... Be careful out there."

He smiled. "I won't be long."

CHAPTER 7

I was bent over in the bedroom with my ass in the air and my skirt riding high on my hips, carefully searching through every drawer for something I could use to get away. He *had* to have a mobile phone somewhere. A spare. Or an old one, at the very least. I couldn't stay here. Not after I'd recognised a temper in him when he cut dinner short. Not only did I not like it, but experience had taught me to be careful of men like Grady.

Men who could dominate me.

Men who could control me.

Men who could melt my very resolve by indiscriminately appealing to my inner femininity.

I couldn't surrender to another one. Not like this. Not in the middle-of-nowhere.

I went to a third chest of drawers, and again sifted through his clothes. I was surprised to see so many varieties. Contrary to my original opinion, Grady had very good clothes. Clothes I'd find him even more attractive in-

I told myself to shut up.

I couldn't think of him that way. He was a bully, and perhaps a brutal one at that. Did I really want to find out what physical abuse could be like? I'd already suffered enough mentally from more than one ex.

But then I thought of his sensitive side. How he'd rescued me. Then taken me out of my soaking wet clothes to save my health and put me in his bed, under warm covers. How he'd provided me with clothes I was secretly thrilled to be wearing. And, most of all, how he was an only child, devoted to his mother. That he was risking life and limb to go from his cottage to hers to make sure she was okay.

I rummaged faster, fearing he could walk back into his home at any minute.

Water splashed on the window.

I realised I'd no idea what direction he'd left in. For all I knew, he could be watching me right now.

I pulled my skirt up to my waist.

The final chest of drawers turned up nothing.

I crawled on all fours to his wardrobe, then started to look inside.

There were shirts and jackets, some leather and well-worn, but nothing which helped my predicament.

I reached behind to scratch my butt cheek, slipping my fingertips into my panties to reach the itchiest region.

What if I found a spare set of keys for his tractor? No! I'd already almost lost my life in that storm once, I wasn't going to risk it again. Even if I wasn't particularly out of danger in Grady's company.

I got through the last of his shirts. I sighed. I'd searched everywhere, and there was no sign of any type of phone. Perhaps he really did just live a quiet life out here, away from all the bullshit-

I saw two boxes, one next to the other, stuffed in at the back of the wardrobe.

My pulse beat faster. I just knew I'd found *something*.

I pulled the first box out to the floor, paused to listen, then opened it.

"Oh my God," I said aloud.

It was Grady's porn collection. Literally anywhere from fifty to a hundred DVDs. I looked through a few, and quickly gathered what they all had in common. He had a simple fetish for shemales and transsexuals, either with each other, alone or with men.

My heart was pounding.

Was this what he wanted from me? To be his chick with a dick?

I thought for a moment. I *kind of* liked it.

My little penis poked at the front of my panties.

Okay, I completely liked it. I'd experimented with dressing up for a guy in lingerie before, and I'd never had a guy cum so quickly. Unfortunately, he was married and I was wearing his wife's gear. I never saw him again for a repeat performance.

I studied the covers. These *gurls* were beautiful. Could I ever look as convincing as that? What if I disappointed Grady? I wanted to please him-

I told myself to behave.

Escape was my priority.

I put the DVDs back in the box, then returned it to the wardrobe.

I lifted out the other, and immediately noticed the stark difference in weight. What was in here?

I panted the moment I opened it.

Everything inside both frightened and excited the absolute hell out of me!

It was like an A-Z of every kinky toy a professional pervert could have on their wish list – An arm-binder, a metal anal hook, a ball gag, a ball lock, blindfolds, a butt plug, chastity belts and cock rings, handcuffs, a bondage harness and hook, a muzzle gag, rope, whips. Not to forget a whole range of different sized dildos!

I was breathless.

He was twice my age, into sissies who cross-dressed or downright became shemales, and he had me at his mercy... There was no way Grady would let me go!

I heard footsteps in the gravel outside!

It had to be him!

I quickly closed the box and shoved it into the wardrobe.

Then I ran out to the kitchen on my stilettos, making a racket on the tiled floor, and grabbed the plates, spinning around and planting them in the sink-

As the front door opened, and a massive gust of wind accompanied his return.

"Bloody hell!" he yelled, forcing the door shut again behind him.

"Your mother okay?" I asked, fixing my skirt back below my ass.

Grady looked at the table.

I inhaled.

"Maxine?"

I exhaled.

"What have you been doing?"

I looked to the table. His cutlery, the pot I'd served the spaghetti bolognese from and the tray I'd set it on were all still in place... As were the condoms.

"Maxine?" he demanded. "Answer me immediately. What have you been up to in my home, while I've been out?"

CHAPTER 8

"Nothing," I whispered, and twirled quickly to retrieve the forgotten items.

"Nothing?" he said. "Sweetheart, do you think I was born yesterday? Nothing never means nothing."

I was trembling. "Grady, please don't do this."

He walked slowly towards me. "Do what?"

I tossed his knife and fork into the kitchen sink. "I... I nearly died."

He nodded.

"I needed a few minutes to myself."

He reached the table.

"I needed to collect my thoughts."

Grady nodded again. "You were taking your time? Okay." He pointed to the condoms. "But you shouldn't have left those sitting out. Didn't you think that anyone could've walked in and seen them?"

Who? His mother? I dared not mention her again, and suspected he was testing me to see if I would.

"Pick them up," he snapped.

I hurried across the tiled floor.

He feasted his eyes on my legs.

I grabbed the condoms.

"Bring them to me, Maxine."

I held all three out to him.

Grady took them from me. "A girl dressed like you shouldn't be trusted with these."

"I know," I muttered, looking down.

Grady stuffed them in his pocket. "My mother's fine, thanks for asking."

Somehow I found myself smiling up to him.

He gestured to the kitchen sink. "Now, hurry up and finish washing the dishes. You're the woman of the house now. You have your duties."

"Yes, Grady." I turned away from him, and quickly set about washing up.

He stood for several seconds. "Has anyone ever told you, Maxine, that you have a nice ass?"

My penis pulsated within my tight panties. "What?"

"You heard me."

"Er..."

"Look at me when I ask you an intimate question," he commanded.

I kept my body facing the sink, my hands scrubbing the plates, but I looked over my shoulder at him.

Grady had one hand in his pocket, seemingly adjusting his balls.

"I've been told I have... An *incredible* ass."

Grady grinned.

I turned my attention to the dishes again.

His eyes burned into all parts of my body.

I felt myself tingle from my toes up, surging straight to my sex.

"Who were you out here trying to meet?" he asked.

I restrained myself from sighing. "Grady, we've been over this-"

"And I know you're holding back."

I breathed carefully out.

"I know you're *lying*."

I looked at him again.

"I've brought you a treat from my mother's. I think you'll like it. In fact, I *know* you will, Maxine, but in order to earn it I want the truth from you."

I glanced to the front door.

"Feel free to leave if you don't like my house rules, baby."

Baby?

"*What* were you doing out here in the country by yourself, Maxine, your body all smooth but for your Brazilian bikini wax?"

I felt a throbbing within my rear. A constant which reminded me of my yearning. "I don't know if I can trust you," I said finally.

"You can't," he snapped. "I'm a total stranger... But I saved your life... You can at least depend on that."

I was afraid of saying the wrong thing, but I knew those looks and I heard his complements. Despite my initial doubts, never mind the DVDs and the toys in his bedroom, this man wanted me. "Will you judge me?"

Grady shook his head.

I scrubbed mince from his knife. "You've obviously worked out my sexuality, right?"

"I want to hear you say it." He approached me from behind.

I felt his breath on the back of my neck, and sensed his groin only an inch or so behind my rear. "I... I'm attracted to men."

"I know."

"But I'm single."

He leaned his chin onto my shoulder. "Really?"

I felt my body heat soar. "I was lonely."

He placed his palms to either side of my tiny waist. "Go on."

"I went online... To meet someone."

He gripped me tighter. "For casual sex?"

I inhaled the most anxious of breaths. "I don't know... Maybe."

"You brought condoms."

"They were precautions," I insisted. "I don't think I'd have gone all the way... Not with a stranger."

He tapped my right side with his forefinger. "I'm a stranger, Maxine."

I hesitated, then dared myself to go further. "No, not quite. I know more about you than some of the men I've slept with."

Grady was silent.

I wondered if he was dumbstruck, or disgusted. "The thing is... These random hook-ups... They do nothing for my self-esteem."

"You feel like a whore afterwards?" he asked, pressing his mouth right to my ear.

I was taken aback. "Grady."

"Say it if it's true."

"I... I feel like a slut."

His grip tightened.

Had I just turned him on with that word? "I don't want to feel like a slut with a random guy..."

"You want to feel like a slut with...?"

I closed my eyes. "Someone special."

Grady removed his hands from my body.

"I... I like dressing up for you," I confessed, even though I was fearful of him too.

He took his head away from me.

"Do... Do you like me dressing up for you, Grady?"

He slapped his palm on the counter.

My eyes shot open.

"This is your treat," he said, then removed his hand to reveal make-up. "You've earned it with your honesty."

I took a deep breath.

"I want you to finish washing up, then go to the bathroom and put on as much make-up as you see fit."

But it was late. I was exhausted. And I'd had a traumatic experience. I wanted to go to sleep.

"Have you worn make-up before, Maxine?"

"No." Yet I knew I'd pacify him in any way possible.

Grady walked to the living room. "You'll be a natural. And a looker too, I bet."

I studied the box of make-up.

"You did say you enjoy dressing up for me," he said, spreading himself eagle on the sofa. "You should get a kick out of this too."

But what if I looked ridiculous? I already knew he'd be comparing me to the beautiful transsexuals in his DVD collection. How could I measure up on my first go?

CHAPTER 9

I felt I was flying blind without my mobile to check online for tips, as I sat in front of the bathroom mirror.

Grady was pacing outside in the hall.

I'd locked the door on him.

First, I washed my face. It seemed the natural thing to do. What better way to start than with a clean, blank canvas?

I pressed three of my fingers into a light foundation, then applied them in turn to spots on my forehead and cheeks. I liked what I saw, so I put one more on my nose and my chin. Then I rubbed them all in, immediately seeing the improvement to my complexion. I didn't want to be too over-the-top, so I tried my best to blend the foundation into my natural skin tone.

I was already enjoying myself, and reached between my legs to rub my erection through my tight cotton panties. "Mmmmmm."

"You okay in there?" Grady said.

"Yes."

"You need a hand?"

"No, Grady, you can see me when I'm finished." I lifted my little length over the top of my panties. "Go read your paper or something."

After several seconds, he trotted off down the hall.

I had plenty of friends who were girls and I'd watched them do their make-up many, many times, so it was really becoming a question of how much attention had I been paying.

I looked tired under my eyes, and far from sexy. So I found a small brush and some concealer, which I gently applied to the inner and outermost parts of the circles under my eyes. I used a sponge to smooth out the rest and the results were instantaneous, changing my look from one of lethargy to lighting up with pizazz.

I decided to go for a light blue eyeshadow next. Something about the shade just spoke of feminine sexuality, and I hoped Grady would approve.

I wasn't heterosexual, but I still appreciated female beauty. Hell, some of my earliest memories were of my mother remarking how she knew only one person who loved Marilyn Monroe more than my sister – me! So I was feeling my inner confidence grow when I started to like what I saw in the mirror. I gave myself another quick fondle.

The blue eyeshadow complemented the structure of my brow bones, and that's where I led the strokes of my little brush from my eyelids.

I wasn't sure about the eyeliner, but I had to try. Girls looked sexier with it than without it, so I hoped I would too. I tried only a little of a dark shade on the rim of each lash line, then I looked away for several seconds, trying to forget what it looked like. Then I looked back... And, from the fresher perspective, I liked what I saw.

I pulled my panties down to my knees.

I reasoned mascara was the next step, and found what I assumed to be the correct wand. I was doing this instinctually. God, this all felt so sexy. How had I never properly done this before? It was such fun, transforming myself to another sex.

I let my panties fall to my feet.

I was in danger of getting carried away with the mascara, as the results were so stark and obvious. I felt like a vamp. Or a seductress.

I squeezed my erection.

I forced myself to stop applying more, and set down the wand. I *really* liked the way I looked.

And the way I felt inside. *Deep* inside. All the way to the walls of my anus.

I returned my attention to the make-up, and found blusher. I dabbed it gently onto my high cheekbones, trying to blend it in. It would've been all too tempting to go overboard and give myself a ridiculous glow, but I wanted Grady to be impressed with me. Not to be guffawing at me.

I crossed my legs, trapping my penis between my thighs. It was the only way I could resist masturbating some of the tension away.

I glanced between the mirror and the make-up, relishing my chance to put on the finishing touch. I'd experimented with this before, more times than I could remember, when I was younger, borrowing my sister's.

I puckered my lips-

"You're very quiet in there," Grady said, sounding as if he'd sneaked right up to the other side of door.

I shushed him. "I'm getting ready. Go wait and be patient." My voice was as girly as my appearance.

He cleared his throat. "I hope you're not masturbating in there."

I said nothing.

"I'll know."

I listened as he walked back down the hall to the living room, then I put my lips back together, as if ready to deliver a kiss, and dabbed the bright red lipstick to the middle of my upper and lower lips. I loved the sluttiness of the colour, but I wouldn't say to Grady in case this make-up really had belonged to his mother. I ran the lipstick across both my upper and lower lips, then quickly realised I'd used too much. I decided to try to smooth the rest out over the remaining parts of my lips, seeking a subtly form of sex appeal.

I clenched my thighs tighter on my sex. The temptation to stroke myself was intensifying, but I heeded Grady's warning. My panties remained around my ankles.

A heavy gust of wind blew against the bathroom window, as I smacked my lips together and took a final glance in the mirror.

I turned first to one side, then the other, eventually striking several poses before I stood up, then stood back, taking in all I could see. I raised my skirt at the front, and compared the image before me to the DVD covers I'd seen in Grady's bedroom.

My heart was beating faster and my erection was pulsating.

I bent down to pull up my panties, stretching them around my penis and forcing it into place.

I fixed my skirt too.

I looked to the mirror. My arousal was barely noticeable.

I unlocked the bathroom door, then stepped out into the hall. There was no sign of Grady.

"I'm finished," I said, nervously.

"Come show me, Maxine. I'm in the living room."

I walked one stiletto-heeled foot in front of the other, deliberately accentuating my femininity from my footwork through to a sassy sway of my hips.

I hoped so much he'd approve.

I walked into the living room, and saw Grady sat on the edge of the sofa.

He looked up to me.

I paused.

He stared.

I froze.

His jaw dropped.

I felt myself judged from head-to-toe.

He ran his eyes all over my face again. He stood. Then he came closer, seemingly assessing every effort I'd made to look good for him.

I knew I couldn't be as hot as one of those transsexuals, but before I'd left the bathroom I'd believed I'd come pretty damned close-

"Maxine," he said slowly.

"Yes, Grady? What do you think?"

He pointed right at my crotch. "What do *you* think, Maxine?"

I hesitated. Was he really pointing at my-

"I think you like dressing up as a girl. Do you?"

I swallowed, then I shyly nodded.

He grinned.

I had to know. "Do..." The suspense was killing me. "Do you like what you see, Grady?" I looked down, fearful of rejection. "Do you think I'm convincing?"

"Yes, I do think you're convincing." He was within touching distance of my body. "I'm stunned, Maxine." He put his forefinger under my chin, raising my head until I looked him in the eye. "I think it's time for bed now."

<u>CHAPTER 10</u>

I felt myself leak precum into my cotton panties as I stood before him. "Bedtime?"

"Yes, Maxine, I'm sure you've heard of it in the big smoke."

But I'd only just put my make-up on.

"Us country folk do an honest day's work on the farm, and we sure need to head to bed to get a night's rest before another."

Lightning lit up the whole living room and kitchen area.

"Of course, Grady," I said, glancing to the sofa and at a particularly cosy looking throw. I knew there was only one bedroom, and only one bed, in the whole cottage. "I'll sleep there."

"Honey, didn't you hear what I said? I said we need to head to bed to get a rest before another day of honest, hard work... I expect you to pull your weight too, if the weather eases."

I was certain I'd be on my way first thing. "You know I will," I insisted, all the same.

"You're missing my point, beautiful..."

I couldn't conceal my smiles at his every complement.

"After the effort you've gone to with your outfit and your make-up, I won't hear of having you on the couch. It's much too cold for a lady like you." He leaned his nose within touching distance of mine. "You're coming to sleep in *my* bed."

Wait? On my own?

Grady took my hand.

With him? What if I didn't want-

He led me out of the living room into the hall.

I followed diligently behind, fixing my skirt into a more respectable position down my thighs as my penis bobbed up and down. I was horny, yet horrified at the prospect of finding myself trapped in this stranger's bed.

Grady held the bedroom door open for me, and gestured for me to enter.

I saw the duvet was already pulled half-way down the bed, on both sides, which was not the way I'd left it earlier.

He slammed the door shut behind me.

I almost jumped.

Thunder rolled nearby.

Grady eyed me like an animal surveying its prey.

I rubbed the back of one leg, just above my sock, with my other foot. I held my hands nervously in front of my groin, guarding my penis and twiddling my thumbs.

"You've gotten shy all of a sudden," he said. "I like that." He nodded. "It's cool." He lifted the front of his checked shirt, then unbuckled the belt of his jeans. "Ah well, you showed me yours, I guess."

I hadn't. He'd stripped me when I was unconscious... I stopped that thought, then tried to reason with myself... He'd done it so I wouldn't catch pneumonia.

"Now let me show you mine."

I couldn't peel my eyes away as Grady unzipped his fly, then let his jeans fall to his ankles.

He stepped out of them, then made me wait as he slowly unbuttoned his shirt one stubborn button after the other, the threads of his worked shirt catching almost all of them and delaying the process.

I stared at his tight, black underwear, making out some of his bulge. Neither the colour of the material nor the lighting of the room made it easy to tell for sure, but I was pretty sure-

"You ready, Maxine?" he asked.

I throbbed in my panties. "Yes."

"You ready to see my cock?"

I nodded.

"Say it."

I thought of the sex toys in his wardrobe. "I want to see it, Grady."

He grinned, then slipped his thumbs into his waistband and pulled his underwear down.

I gawped at his girth.

He didn't check my reaction, as if he was so self-assured he didn't need to.

I was in giddy awe.

He probably knew it.

I stood with my legs tight together.

Grady folded his clothes, then threw his boxers into a basket in the corner. He turned to face me. "I sleep naked, do you mind?"

Mind? Was he kidding? My eyes were all over the muscles of his working man's body. "That's fine, Grady. It's your home."

"It is."

"What side do you take?" I asked.

He pointed to the nearest.

I walked around the end of the bed, breezing my hand past his groin and resisting the natural instinct to reach out and touch.

Grady got into bed first.

I started to join him on the other side.

"What are you doing?" he demanded.

I froze, timid beyond belief at his tone. "I'm sorry?"

"You should be. Those are good clothes which belonged to my cousin's daughter. I let you wear them in the good faith that you'd take care of them, Maxine. Would you sleep in good clothes you'd spent your own money on?"

I was silent.

"Well?"

"No, Grady," I said. "I'm sorry." But what the hell was I going to sleep in? I couldn't just sleep naked next to him. I knew what I was like. I'd-

"If you're too shy to sleep like me, you can wear the underwear." He smiled. "But I'm watching you strip." He propped himself up by his elbow, gazing at me, waiting.

I gave the window a momentary glance. There weren't any curtains. What if his mother came over early when the storm lifted? Or a postman?

Grady slipped one hand under the duvet.

I couldn't tell for sure if it was on his cock.

Surely nothing was going to happen between us with the window being so open, right?

I slid my knees off the bed, and stood for him to watch.

His forearm was still.

I gently pulled my white blouse out from the waist of my skirt, then undid the buttons. "Do you like my tight waist?" I asked, daring set myself up for a scornful rejection.

"Yes," he said, somewhat hoarsely.

I watched for movement again from his arm, as I removed my blouse.

"Your whole body is so slim..."

I recalled his complement of my ass, and tried to make it look innocent as I turned my back to him.

"And sexy."

I reached behind for the little zip on my pleated skirt. I lowered it slowly, then shimmied my hips until it fell.

Grady wolf-whistled.

I pulled my panties higher and tighter, more of the material sinking between my buttocks and revealing more ass.

I looked over my shoulder at him. "My feet get cold at night."

He said nothing.

I turned, and set one foot on the bed. I pointed at my sexy, frilly sock. "I want to keep these on."

Grady nodded profusely.

I drew back the duvet, much more than necessary.

His hand wasn't on his cock, nor was it fully erect.

I had to be careful not to pant as I looked at it. I found it so very attractive. Quite fat. With definitely a lot to work with. And I really wanted to know how long it grew to.

Gray lay down on his back.

I slid next to him on my side, but I left a reasonable, short distance.

He said nothing.

I felt a little silly in my bra, without any titties for him to admire, but my make-up kept my self-confidence up.

Grady closed his eyes.

I felt disappointment crash over all parts of me like waves hitting rocks on the coast. Was this really all he wanted?

He sighed.

What? What!? What!?!

He breathed normally.

I pulled the duvet over my chest.

Grady turned in bed to look at me. His eyes were all over my face, taking in my make-up.

"What is it?" I whispered, knowing I'd put my hand on his cock if he told – or asked – me to.

"Max, Maxine, can I ask you a question?"

I used all my inner resolve to hide my delight. "Of course."

"I'm sorry, but... How'd your mother die?"

I hesitated. It'd been years, but it was still raw to me. It always would be. "Leukaemia."

The window behind me shook in the wind.

Grady took my face in his hands. "I wish that'd never happened to you."

"Thank you."

"I mean that. I know I've just met you, and you probably think I'm some crazy country man..."

I shook my head. I thought he was sex on legs.

"But I've always been a good judge of character. And I think you, Maxine, are one of the loveliest people I've ever met."

I was red-faced.

"You are," he said, then he pressed his lips on mine.

I was caught unexpectedly, thrown by the comment about my mother, and didn't know what to do at first.

He pressed further.

I wanted to open my mouth to return a proper kiss-

Grady retreated.

I'd missed my moment before I even realised it was there.

"I can't imagine what that must've been like," he said, lying on his back again and staring at the ceiling.

I exhaled.

"Seriously, if you want to leave..." He placed his arms over the duvet. "Just leave."

I inhaled.

"How do you feel?" he asked.

I took a second, then rested my left arm over both of his. "I feel safe." I snuggled myself against his side. "I don't want to leave, Grady."

CHAPTER 11

I awoke only once from my sleep all night, and by that time it was early morning and daylight.

I still felt a little tired, yet rested all the same. My bones were no longer sore from lying in the floodwater, nor did my muscles ache.

Rain lashed the window behind me. Strong winds still blew. The storm had entered another day.

I felt at the bare spot on the other side of the bed. Where was Grady so early? Perhaps off flexing those spectacular muscles, moving more heavy trees that'd fallen overnight.

I rolled over, and looked out the window.

Someone was crouching down, staring right at me.

My heart raced.

The person was wearing a black hat and covering most of the rest of their face.

But the piercing glance of those eyes shocked me.

They bolted suddenly off out of sight.

I had my hand on my chest, clutching. Who the hell was that? I was shaking. Why didn't Grady have curtains? I felt afraid and so unsafe. What if that person tried to get in? What if they attacked me for who I was?

Some of my make-up had smudged on the pillow overnight.

I was sure I looked a whorish mess, even though nothing sexual had happened between us.

Clouds covered the sky above.

I lowered my legs out of bed onto the cool floor, then cautiously approached the window, fearful that person – I wasn't even sure if it was male or female – was still in the garden. I looked down, checking they weren't crouching underneath, then out to see if they were visible among the hedges or between the trees. I couldn't see them. I noticed one tree was down.

I was still frightened as I looked around the room for a dressing gown. I couldn't see one. I didn't feel like immediately dressing up as a schoolgirl again, so I walked around the bed and out to the hall in my bra, panties and ankle socks, checking every window I could in case that person was there.

"Grady?" I called out.

No answer.

I walked into the living room and kitchen area.

There was no sign of him.

I glided into the kitchen, found the kettle and filled enough water for two cups in case Grady came back soon.

I checked the front door was securely locked. It was, but I felt only a fraction safer.

Why was someone spying on me? Had they been able to work out my gender from outside? Or did they know Grady, and they were so desperately nosy they needed to know who was in his bed?

The kettle slowly boiled.

I decided to head for the bathroom to retouch my make-up, as I wondered if that person had been his mother. I sincerely hoped it hadn't. Somehow I got the impression the mother of a 42-year-old, only child, country boy wouldn't be the most forward-thinking, tolerant of women.

I returned to the kitchen twenty minutes later with my face freshened and both my crotch and my rear scrubbed clean. I doubted it was necessary, but I prided myself on my hygiene and especially so now I was – albeit temporarily until the storm lifted – living the life of a girl.

I sat down at the table, nursing a cup of tea and trying to calm my nerves.

Those piercing, seething *eyes.*

I tapped the table.

Watching, staring, judging-

The front door opened.

I sat up in my bra and panties, ready to run... Where exactly? To the bathroom, where there was a lock! And then wait for this evil stalker to break the door down and...

There were heavy footsteps.

Murder me!

"Grady!" I shouted, leaping to my feet.

He smiled.

I ran to him and threw my arms around him. "I'm so glad it's you!"

His strong arms went around my back. "Of course it's me,

sweetie. How'd you sleep?"

I looked up to his gorgeous blue eyes. "Sleep? Uh, great. But, Grady, there was-"

"I'm glad to hear it." He let go of me, then walked back out to the little enclave where the front door was. "The storm's still on, but I was able to make it up to my mother's. I got some things for you and I've got a suggestion for the day."

I stared at him. He seemed so positive. So focused. But I had to tell him.

He set down two bags. "What is it, Maxine? What's wrong?"

I watched his demeanour slowly, then swiftly, differ. "Grady, someone was here."

"Someone was *here*?" He gestured to the room.

I placed my hands on my hips. "Not right here."

He looked down on me.

I already felt silly, but I knew what I saw. "I was in the bedroom. I'd just woken up. Someone was at the window."

Grady laughed at me.

"There was!"

He put his palm on my little shoulder, and gave me a playful squeeze. "You're so cute, Maxine. Baby, you were dreaming."

I shook my head. "I saw them, Grady! I know I did. They were wearing a black hat and covering their face-"

"They?"

I hesitated.

"What is it, Maxine?"

I felt awkward, and fixed my panties higher. "They ran off when they realised I saw them."

"They? Them? How many were there?"

I looked to the kitchen, to the kettle. "I couldn't tell if it was male or female."

He laughed again, louder.

I turned to walk away.

Grady held me. "Wait, wait, wait. Sweetheart, please, I'll take a look around the property when you've fixed me a coffee. But rest assured you must've imagined it. No one would be out in this weather."

"You were."

He flexed his muscles under his shirt. "Because I've never been scared of man nor beast in my entire life, baby."

I walked to the kettle, and flicked it back on.

It was his mother. He was covering for her.

"Grady, I'm not meaning to sound rude or disrespectful, but is your mother housebound?"

He steeled his teeth between his lips, then noisily hauled out a chair at the kitchen table.

All I wanted was a straight answer.

"I told you not to talk to me about her."

So was she or wasn't she? Had she even been in her cottage when he called over? I had to find out more about her.

"Go grab those two bags and bring them here," he barked. "They're not heavy."

As I walked on the tiled floor of the kitchen I was really beginning to miss my stilettos, as the cold got to my feet. I lifted the bags.

Grady took them from me. "Tell me this, Maxine, I like my sissies with pierced ears-"

I giggled. "I know you do."

He shot daggers at me. "What's that supposed to mean?"

I shrugged, playing dumb.

He studied me. "Are your ears pierced?"

I nodded. "Both of them."

Grady smiled. "Brilliant, then these are all for you." He pushed the bag to me. "There's nail varnish in there too."

I looked inside and saw dozens of pairs of earrings. All different styles and colours. I started to lift some out to examine them.

"I like the big slutty ones the best."

I knew, I'd seen those DVD covers.

"Hooped," he added.

I found the perfect gold pair, which were probably bigger than my little ears, and held them up to him.

"Put them on, Maxine."

I did exactly as I was told. I took one glance at Grady, then knew I'd to pose for him, slowly turning my head like a model for a camera.

"You're making me hard."

Was I? Could I see? I was desperate to know what his big, fat cock looked like fully erect.

"Aren't you curious to know what's in the other bag?"

"I'm afraid," I said, joking after what I'd found yesterday in the wardrobe.

He narrowed his eyebrows. "What's so funny?"

"Nothing, Grady, I'm just joking. I'm nervous-"

"Why? Was I not a gentleman with you in my bed last night?"

"Totally," I insisted.

"Did I respect your boundaries?"

"Yes, Grady, yes!"

He put his hand on the bag. "Perhaps I should take these back, and let you freeze in your undies."

"You brought me more clothes!?!" I instinctively put my fingers on his wrist. "Please, let me see! I'm dying to dress up in *anything* you pick out for me!"

Grady took his hand away. "I only brought you one outfit."

I opened the bag.

"I hope it's not *too* dignified."

CHAPTER 12

I felt his eyes all over me as I bent over to pick up his laundry basket. "Y'know, when I was looking for the person who looked in on me..."

He sighed. "It was your imagination, Maxine."

"No, it wasn't. Anyway, I saw a tree down out back."

"I know, and I'm on it," he insisted.

I deliberately rotated my rump. "Really? It looks to me like you're just sitting there watching me... *Perving* on me, in fact."

"It's my house, Maxine. My rules. I set them. And I set the chores. You keep up your cheek and I'll send you out to deal with that tree."

I lifted the basket, twirled on my stilettos, and looked at him. "You'd really send me out there to dirty my new outfit?"

Grady shook his head.

I smiled, glad he saw sense.

"I'd strip you out of it first..."

My smile dropped with my jaw.

"Your underwear too."

I was frozen on the spot.

"In fact, you interrupted me when I first got back from mother's. Didn't you hear me say I had a suggestion? And, to be honest, your underwear doesn't match your dress. It's distracting, Maxine."

"Right... Okay, Grady." I felt my body shrink under his watchful eyes. "What was your suggestion?" I knew I'd do it no matter what, even as my imagination drifted to those implements I'd found in his wardrobe.

"I believe today should be a no panties day."

I gulped.

He undid his belt and lowered his jeans. "I'll even remove my boxer shorts, so you're not the odd one out."

I stood in a shoulderless, red lace, gold-sequinned professional dancer's dress, cut-away so deep at the back it revealed almost all my spine to my rear, and stopped so short it barely touched the top of my thighs.

"Don't be shy, Maxine, I've seen you all before."

I slipped my fingers under my dress, then pulled my cotton panties away from my crotch, freeing my sex. I dragged them down, then stepped out of them. I unhooked my bra, and tugged it out as well.

"I'm curious about that." He was pointing between my legs. "What'd you call her?"

"*Her*?" I asked.

"That little thing there." Grady adjust his massive shaft in front of me. "What do you refer to it as?"

"My penis."

Grady laughed. "Don't be ridiculous. That's not a penis. It's not a dick. And it's certainly not a cock."

I was at a loss.

He kicked his boxers in the air, and they landed right in my laundry basket. "That right there," he said, his forefinger in line with my sex, "is your clit, do you understand me, Maxine?"

"Yes, Grady... My clit."

"Good." He pulled his jeans back up.

Wait?

He buckled his belt.

"I thought this no panties day was going to be both of us."

"It is," he said. "And we're both wearing clothes."

I strutted off to the washing machine in the kitchen, feeling my clit swing from thigh to thigh, visible beneath my short dress. There was no way he'd got this dress from his mother's. It couldn't be hers. My suspicions were magnifying that she didn't even live there. Perhaps there wasn't another cottage at all. Maybe he had a shed or a barn where he stored the clothes of previous... Victims? And the man in the hat was his accomplice? Yet, I couldn't be sure it was a man. I'd already suspected it was his mother.

Grady was stood looking out the living room window at the storm.

"Would your mother need any washing done?" I asked.

"No."

"It'd be no trouble for me to wash clothes from her cottage as well."

"I told you not to mention her, Maxine."

I had to find an excuse to get up there, if *there* even existed at all.

He walked towards the hall.

"So, Grady, when did you first know you liked girls like me?"

He stopped.

"Y'know, chicks with dicks-"

"It's a clit," he snapped.

I leaned my back against the washing machine, and parted my legs. "Oops, silly me... So when did you first find yourself attracted to transsexuals?"

He narrowed his eyes on me.

I flicked my clit.

He stared, his chest inflating.

"Tell me... What is it you like so much about... Shemales?"

His foot thudded on the floor.

I shut my legs.

He raced across the room.

Oh fuck!

"I'm going back to my mother's for a bit," he said, almost snarling. "Make sure you've finished your chores by the time I get back."

I nodded, too scared to say anything.

His heavy feet stopped in the enclave.

I waited, my pulse pounding.

He wasn't moving.

Why hadn't he gone out the front door? Or even made a move for his coat?

A floorboard creaked as he set one foot back in the living room.

I looked innocently over to him. "Yes?"

He glared at me. "Tell me the truth, and I won't be mad."

I stretched the front of my dress below my clit.

"Have you been snooping around my home while I've been out?"

I was too terrified to tell him the truth. "No!"

He winked at me. "Okay, then." His smile returned. "I won't be long."

I swiped perspiration from my forehead, as he turned back to the enclave. That'd been close. Too close. And, me being me, it'd only have taken him to ask me just once more if I was sure and I'd have confessed the truth and thrown myself at his mercy.

Grady slammed the front door behind him.

I knew I'd probably not get another chance, and walked out to the enclave. I found a huge, spare winter jacket and wrapped it around my body. Then swapped my stilettos for a pair of his ridiculously bigger, heavy boots.

The sound of his footsteps were already slipping out of earshot.

I stood on my tiptoes and looked out the tiny window at the top of the door.

Grady was almost out of sight.

I put my palm on the doorknob. I took a deep breath. Then I dared walk out behind him.

CHAPTER 13

The rain thudded heavier than ever, as I kept my distance from Grady on the tiny, winding, mucky path which started on the edge of his property and now led between two tall hedges. There was a little respite from the wind, but still the temperature must've been biting close to zero. I hauled his jacket tighter around my body, however the zip was broke so I couldn't properly seal it at the front.

I felt as if someone was dropping ice on my head, hands and legs, then looked up and saw the rain was turning to sleet.

My body wanted to turn back, to admit defeat to this bitterness.

Grady walked at pace onwards.

I wiped moisture from my cheeks, then cursed my running mascara.

There were crows watching from the trees and a bat swooping between them.

Grady whistled, using his fingers, as if to grab someone else's attention.

I crouched down low beside a hedge, hoping I'd be hidden enough to be unseen.

He kept walking.

No one whistled back.

I watched.

The sleet was slipping under the collar of my jacket, freezing the bare skin of my back.

I wanted to go back. What had I to learn from following him to his mother's cottage?

If he was hiding something that could endanger your life.

I got to my feet and started following him again.

The path was beginning to open up ahead, where Grady was.

My pulse was beating so hard I could hear it within my own head, as if my veins were bloating and banging against my brain. All he had to do was hear one sound out of place or sense one thing that'd make him look around and he'd see me. I was putting myself in danger, and especially after I'd just lied to him about snooping through his things.

I got a sudden mental picture of his plethora of dildos.

He started up some concrete steps.

I stopped, then followed him only with my eyes.

The steps led to the gate of another property. A cottage.

I breathed carefully out. Was this his mother's place? Had he been telling the truth all along?

He turned to shut the gate behind him.

I was already shielding myself beneath the hedge.

His boots trampled the concrete path.

I walked quietly on the mud, bringing myself closer to the steps.

There was the sound of a door being loudly shut.

I waited at the bottom of the steps, and listened.

Nothing.

I slowly climbed them, keeping the noise of my boots to a minimum, until the cottage came into my eyesight. I kept myself low, as I tried to work out if I could get closer to the building without being seen.

The path from the steps led straight to the front door. There was a single window to either side of the door. If I walked forward, I'd be totally exposed.

I kept watching.

Suddenly, there was movement inside. It was Grady.

I could easily make him out.

He was holding what looked like a hot water bottle. He lifted another one, then passed the first to an elderly woman.

I realised he wasn't lying. She was obviously his mother. And he was inside there, caring for her, swapping a colder hot water bottle for a warmer one. I looked inside again.

He was stretching. His mother was looking up to him. She wasn't wearing a black hat, and didn't seem particularly able-bodied enough to have been the same person who'd spied on me in the bedroom.

I had to get back before I caught cold out here.

Grady looked right at me.

I froze, hoping the gate would obscure his vision enough to-

He ran suddenly for the front door.

I sprinted off down the steps and back onto the path.

CHAPTER 14

Sleet slammed into my face. Icy cold water splashed off my boots and onto my legs, muddying my skin.

I dared look behind me.

Panic plundered every sense of safety which seeing him care for his mother had brought only moments earlier.

Grady didn't say or shout anything. He didn't need to.

My terrible fear was in knowing he was right behind me.

And I was alone. With no one else around. Not even a spying stranger in a black hat. I'd nowhere to turn for help.

Floodwater was flowing down either side of the lane.

My little clit flopped about beneath Grady's jacket.

I tried to stomp a faster path in his bigger boots.

His cottage was within sight.

But what was my plan? To run inside and hide? Or take off into the storm dressed like a transvestite reject from the next Dancing With The Stars?

"Max!" he called from behind.

Not even Maxine.

My mascara dripped onto his jacket.

I ran up to the front door and turned the doorknob. The door wouldn't open. It seemed to have locked itself when I closed it behind me.

Grady was running up behind me.

I turned around. "Grady, please. I–"

"You *were* snooping!" he shouted, as he reached the side of his house.

I'd nowhere to go.

"Not just at my mother's, but here. Today. Or yesterday." He stopped right in front of me, slapping his palms either side of my face on the door.

I was pinned between them.

"You lying, little fucking whore."

Wind cracked across my face.

He grabbed his jacket, and yanked it off me.

I felt the harshness of the storm ten times colder.

"You gave yourself away, Maxine, when you said about the shemales, didn't you?"

I was whimpering.

"Admit it!"

I was coughing on both the cold and on holding back tears. "Yes, Grady."

He hauled out a set of keys, then unlocked the front door. "Get in there," he said, and shoved me forcefully inside. "Take those boots off."

I obeyed him, kicking off the mud-covered footwear.

"Your legs are covered in shit too. And your make-up's a fucking joke." He pushed me out of the enclave into the living room. "Stay here and don't fucking move."

I was shaking, shivering as much from fear as from the intense cold.

Grady stormed up the hall to his bedroom.

My clit was shrivelled under my dress.

Within seconds, he appeared again, carrying one of the boxes I'd found the day before. "You didn't even do a good job at disguising your snooping, you sissy bitch. This box was in the wrong spot to where I hide it."

I wondered why he hid it if his mother was truly housebound.

Grady dumped the box on the kitchen table. "You looked through this?"

I nodded.

"Answer me when I speak to you, Max."

"Yes, Grady, I looked through both boxes. I'm sorry, but... Please don't call me Max... Call me Maxine."

"Shut up," he snapped, looking between me and the box.

I wondered which one it was he'd brought in.

"How dare you go through my stuff when I saved your life and brought you back here out of the storm."

Was it the tame one with the DVDs?

"You wouldn't have survived out there without me. You'd be dead, Maxine. Fucking dead."

Or the one with all the horrific sexual toys and bondage implements?

"And how dare you judge me," he continued. "Don't give me that innocent look, sweetheart. I'm not a shit-for-brains. I can tell.

You went through my stuff and you had a reaction, didn't you?
Yeah, you did. And did I judge *you*?"

After moments of silence, I gave a slight shrug.

"It hurts, Maxine."

I took one bare-footed step towards him. "What does, Grady?"

"Having my kinks judged."

I shook my head. "I *didn't* judge you, Grady. I'm sorry for lying.
You caught me off guard and I didn't know what to-"

"You didn't follow me to my mother's off guard, did you? No,
you thought you'd risk her seeing you and to hell with what I
wanted. You've hurt me, Maxine. Not just on judging my kinks, but
on abusing my trust... And you know what angers me the most?"

"No," I whispered.

"That I know you were out there in your pink fuck mobile to
meet a guy... A guy you fully intended to fuck..."

My chest filled with anxiety as I breathed deeply in.

"And I've not made you do a single sexual thing with me."

I dared hold his eye in silence. It was true. He hadn't *made* me
do anything.

His gaze strayed to my bare shoulders, then to how the lace
dress clung at my midriff and finally to the gold sequins which led to
the edge and to my clit.

"Don't you want to?" I demanded, and took another step
forward.

He said nothing.

"For God's sake, Grady, answer me. Am I the type of *girl* you'd
want to fuck or not?"

"Yes," he said. "Of course I want to."

I smiled.

"But I don't want to force you."

"I don't feel that way."

He looked at the box. "I'm embarrassed you found these. I'm
humiliated."

I reached for his hand in mine. "What I did was wrong, Grady. I
know that. I shouldn't have had a nosy in your wardrobe. And I
shouldn't have followed you to your mother's. From now on, I'll
respect your boundaries."

Wind whipped at the surrounding walls and the kitchen window
creaked as if it was almost about to crash in on us.

"Grady, I don't want you to be embarrassed. You shouldn't be. If I can stand here dressed like this, covered in mud and with my make-up running... And *still* feel sexy when you look at me that way... There's hope."

"Hope?" he asked.

I hesitated. "Not yet, but can you forgive me?"

He rubbed his thumb on my finger. "If you're truly sorry, Maxine."

"I am." I looked at the box. "Is that the box with the DVDs?"

Grady shook his head.

"Good," I insisted. "It's this box I'm interested in."

He narrowed his eyebrows. "You are?"

I nodded. "Grady, I don't want you to forgive me until I've earned your forgiveness. And I don't think I should be forgiven until I've been punished." I took my hand from his, then pulled my dress up to my hips. "It is no panties day, after all."

He gazed longingly at my little clit.

"Will you punish me, Grady? Will you use some of those terrifying implements I found in your wardrobe?" I flicked my clit. "Will you make me totally submit to you?"

CHAPTER 15

Grady dragged me by my hair and one hand into the enclave.

"You're hurting me!" I squealed, only half-acting, and grabbed my stilettos from the ledge.

He shoved the door open with his shoulder and threw me through.

I stumbled outside on my bare feet, and thought for a moment the door was about to slam in my face.

Grady followed me out, then pulled it shut behind him. He had the box under one arm. "You're shivering, Maxine."

My dress was still up to my hips.

"It makes your clit even smaller."

My breath lit up in the open air. "Can we go back inside, Grady? I'm freezing."

He laughed. "You beg me to punish you, then you ask me to stop after a few seconds out here?" He pulled a cigarette from his shirt pocket, then lit up.

It was the first I'd any inkling he even smoked.

"Special occasions," he remarked, and gave me a wink.

I wondered if I could take that as reassurance.

"Take your dress off, Maxine."

"Grady, no, please-"

"Take it off!"

I looked around, terrified the person in the hat might actually still be watching.

"You imagined him," Grady said, exhaling over me.

Him?

"Take that fucking dress off."

I slipped it down from my arms first, then my torso, hips and thighs until it dropped to the ground. "I'm sorry for humiliating you, Grady-"

"Put your stilettos on."

I stepped quickly into them, but I was otherwise naked as the wind wrapped sleet around my body.

"Let's go," he said, and walked past me.

Before I could turn, he grabbed my hair in a bunch and began dragging me with him. "Grady! Please don't be so rough with me!"

"Shut up, sissy."

I obeyed him.

He led me around the outside of his cottage, past the window at the bedroom.

I felt terribly uneasy as I looked out to the edge of his property, suspecting that's where the person in the black hat had run off to. I covered my crotch.

Grady slammed the box into my abdomen. "Carry this. Use both hands. Hold it high."

I clutched the box at my midriff.

"Higher, slut. Cover your titties. Show off your clit."

In the coldness of the storm, my reddening face was the only part of my skin not turning blue.

"There," Grady snapped, and pointed to a shed in the corner of the garden.

I was thankful only that I'd be out of the cold.

"D'you have a good look in that box, Maxine?"

I couldn't move my head, as his grip tightened on my hair. "I only looked for a minute or two, Grady, I swear... I'm only twenty-one... Most of those things I've never seen before... In person."

"Most," he repeated, laughing as he let go of me. He flicked his cigarette onto the ground, stamped it out and found his keys.

I was glad when he spanked my ass, then shoved me into the shed.

Grady locked the door behind us, then flicked on the light, revealing a standard little shed with tools I couldn't name, tins of oils and paints, dirty towels and a couple of clear white stains on the floor I was immediately suspicious of.

I stood facing him, holding the box, with one stiletto-heeled foot crossed at the ankle in front of the other.

"When did you first know?" he asked.

Huh?

"That I wanted to fuck that tight asshole of yours."

I gasped.

He grinned. "Don't act coy, Maxine. It *is* cute..." He lifted the lid off the box. "But this is neither the time nor the place."

"I'm not sure, Grady. I was kind of in denial. You're extremely masculine... My type."

"Really?" He lifted out a realistic black dildo of eight or more inches.

I nodded. "Except, in my experience, men like you have never been attracted to me..."

His eyes darted to mine.

"Until now. Until I became... Maxine."

"Open your mouth, slut," he barked.

I did as I was-

Grady shoved the dildo into my mouth. "That's it, baby. Suck that cock. Make it wet. Show me your technique."

My clit shot hard.

His eyes grew more lustful, as he moved his head first to one side, then the other, examining how deeply I could take the fake, veiny phallus.

I made muffled murmurs over it, as my saliva spilled down my chin.

Grady shoved it further down to my throat.

I tried not to gag.

"Don't drop that box, Maxine. Concentrate!"

I sucked the rest of my saliva down, slurping at the dildo.

"If you could see yourself now, baby. Your make-up's a slutty, used mess. Your slim, sexy legs are covered in muck... You... You look like a fuck pig."

I moaned into the dildo.

"You like that?" he asked.

I nodded.

He pulled the dildo away from me.

I tried to follow it-

"Stand still!" he yelled.

I froze, panting. "I'm so horny, Grady." I moved the box to show him my sex. "Will you touch me?"

"In what world is touching a girl's clit a punishment?"

I hesitated.

"Exactly, Maxine." He looked into the box. "Any requests?"

I locked my eyes on his.

He looked up, meeting my gaze. "Max-"

"I want to feel like a lowly animal, Grady... A fuck-"

"Pig," he concluded, then slipped his hand into the box. "I hope

you're prepared to get what you ask for."

I smiled. "Yes, Grady, yes."

"Close your eyes."

I closed them.

Grady rummaged through the box. "I don't want you to see what's coming."

My smile widened.

He lifted something out, then he took the box away from me completely. "Keep your eyes shut, fuck pig." He set the box on the floor. "Turn around. Do *not* touch your clit."

My chest inflated with an anxious intake of breath, as I slowly turned away from him on my heels.

Grady grabbed my right ass cheek, and spent several seconds fondling it. "Your skin's so soft."

"Thank you," I said.

He smacked it.

I gasped.

He snatched hold of my left buttock.

I couldn't help it, and moved my ass against his grip.

He slapped me harder, stinging my skin. "Hold still, fuck pig."

"Yes, Grady."

"Open your mouth wide. Make a great big O with your lips." He came right up against my naked rear.

I could feel the warmth of his erection.

Grady set a ball gag in my mouth, then pulled it tight and fastened it around the back of my head. "Some sluts don't deserve a voice, do they?"

I shook my head, as my clit leaked precum.

"Or the use of their hands." He pulled my wrists behind my back, and tightly cuffed them.

I moaned.

"I don't care what you're trying to tell me."

I moaned louder.

Grady unbuckled his belt, then removed it completely.

Oh my God, was he going to beat me with it? I'd fantasised about a real man's man doing this to me before, but I'd never come close to it really happening.

He unzipped his fly, then lowered his jeans. "Keep your eyes shut or I'll blindfold you, fuck pig."

I nodded, then sucked a build-up of saliva from the ball gag.

He stepped out of his jeans.

I wanted desperately to see his big, fat cock again.

He was silent.

I couldn't help myself and tried to feel for him with my fingers.

"Are you trying to find my cock, sissy?"

I nodded profusely. I wanted to *feel* it.

"Who said it would ever be for you?"

I could only listen in frustration as Grady took hold of his length and began to masturbate behind me.

CHAPTER 16

He was really slapping his palm vigorously back and forth on his foreskin.

I mumbled.

He grunted.

I tried again to reach for him with my fingertips.

He patted my ass with his free hand. "No touching for you, sissy. This is your punishment, remember?"

And I found it agonising. It wasn't what I wanted – I'd craved to be spanked and roughly fondled – but it was probably what I deserved.

Grady continued to pummel his rod and playfully, almost condescendingly, pat my rear.

My clit stood firm.

"You better still have your eyes shut, Maxine."

I made a whimpered attempt at confirmation.

"Good girl," he said, and squeezed my left buttock.

I grazed the tip of his cock with my fingernail.

He dug his fingers deep into my flesh until it hurt. "Stop trying to touch me! You haven't earned the right..."

I waited for a *yet* which never came.

He parted my cheeks with his finger and thumb.

I desperately needed to relieve my own sex, but even that paled in comparison to my desires to see and to touch his. He was giving me the ultimate punishment, denying both sight and involvement in bringing him physical pleasure.

Grady pushed my cheeks further apart.

I lifted my cuffed wrists to afford him a better view of my hole.

"Oh fuck," he quipped. "I can't hold on."

I felt a heat born of expectation rise within my own body.

He battered his member behind me.

I made a muffled attempt at asking him where he was going to-

"Shit!" Grady yelled, and ejaculated a volley of his hot sperm onto my tail bone.

My skin sizzled.

He landed more on both my buttocks.

I was excitedly jingling my cuffs up and down.

Grady shot a huge further load on my tail bone, then planted his free hand on my shoulder to steady himself. "I fucking needed that," he groaned.

I was running the fingers of one of my hands over the fingers of the other, trying to manage my temptation to grab him when I could sense his warmth within touching distance.

"You don't mind me cumming on you, do you?"

I vehemently shook my head.

"Good slut," he said, then wiped the rest of his spunk on my cheeks.

I leaked more precum, as I was overcome by the sensations of his shaft on my flesh.

He pulled it away. "Your eyes still shut?"

I nodded.

"I'm not going to clean this cum off you yet, okay?"

I was delighted, and made sure I nodded fast and blatantly, giving him a double thumbs up to be sure.

"My first load landed just above your crack. You can probably feel it sliding down between your cheeks right now."

It felt heavenly.

"You can open your eyes now, Maxine."

I did, and blinked several times to readjust to the light.

"Turn around."

As I rotated myself on my heels, Grady was already back down in his box of tricks, selecting another implement.

I was elated! Did this mean my punishment wasn't done?

"You're getting very excited by all this," he said, and made a nonchalant gesture to my clit. "This should help maintain that." Grady held up a cock ring, then he grabbed my erection.

I looked needily down at him, silently begging for him to masturbate me.

He shoved the ring on my sex, pulling my clit all the way through.

I grimaced at its tightness as he forced it to my base.

Grady ran his fingertips underneath, grazing my scrotum. "You feel full, Maxine. Your little girly balls full of love juice?"

I nodded.

"Do you want to release them?"

My clit pulsated.

He saw it.

I nodded, and made my eyes wide to encourage him.

"Tough." He backhanded my sex. "You begged to be punished. You didn't beg to be brought to orgasm."

I whined, wishing desperately to feel his lips take to my clitoris.

He lifted a butt plug out of the box. "I wonder should I shove this up your ass?" He spat on it. "I really have no idea what your sexual preferences are... I can only guess." He studied my naked body for several seconds. "I wonder how many men have fucked you."

I struggled to stand still.

"Held you down and forced you to take it hard, even when it's hurting you."

I sucked my saliva from the inside of the ball gag, fearful I'd dribble down into the box.

"Do you want this?" he asked, holding the butt plug out for me to examine.

I hesitated.

Grady grabbed me by my thighs, then aggressively twirled me around. "Why am I even asking?"

I whimpered.

He placed it between my buttocks.

I could feel him deliberately wet it with his cum.

Grady pressed the latex head against my rectum.

I grimaced.

He pushed harder.

I gripped one hand with the other.

He made me take it inside.

I sucked at the ball gag for breath.

Grady punched the base of the plug, sending the entirety of the rest right up my rectum.

My cries were suppressed, yet unmistakeable.

He – almost lovingly – stroked my skin, and quietly shushed me.

I tried to regulate my breathing.

Grady stood up behind me. "You are a pretty, little angel. I hope you know that. But this hasn't actually been the majority of your punishment. No, Maxine, this has only been the set-up."

I tried to look over my shoulder at him.

He physically held my head in place, facing directly away from him. "You interrupted me tending to my mother. She's old and she's frail. That was unacceptable, honey."

I tried to say "I'm sorry," but it was impossible.

"I'm going to go back up and see her now." Grady began to pull his jeans back on. "You can wait here for me and reflect on what you've done."

What? Wait here? Alone? In the cold? And naked?

"And one more thing," he said, crouching in the corner to retrieve something. "This was last week's potato sack." He held it up to show me. "I can think of one more use for it." He turned it upside down and placed it over my head.

I was suddenly cloaked in darkness.

"I'll try not to be long." He opened the shed door, and walked out.

I waited. I listened. Why was he wait-

He shut it behind him.

I breathed deeply in, then out. I felt so trapped-

Grady locked me in.

CHAPTER 17

I stood awkwardly on my stilettos, my ankles beginning to feel the brunt of not being used to such footwear.

The wind whistled outside, as if mocking my fate.

I rubbed each of my wrists with the opposing thumbs. The handcuffs were making them itchy.

I wondered how long it'd been since Grady left. An hour? Two?

I could just make out my little clit in the cock ring when I struggled to look down from within the potato sack. I was still so hard, and wanted desperately to wank her. I made out the muck on my legs as well.

I felt so helpless.

And exposed too.

Grady could be watching me from outside, through the window.

I shuddered, the realities of danger rifling through my mind, as I thought of the person in the black hat being out there. He or she could be staring at me right now. Had Grady left the key in the lock? What if their intentions were to do me harm? I could be hit. I could be hurt. I could be sexually abused.

Perhaps I was being filmed!

I tried to turn myself slightly away from the window, shielding my clit from view, but now I was fully exposing the bottom of the butt plug hanging out of my hole.

I was perspiring under the potato sack.

I sucked in errant saliva from the gag.

My stomach rumbled, and I realised I hadn't eaten anything yet.

Tiredness began to take hold of more than my ankles and my wrists. My whole legs were getting sore. My head fuzzy.

Yet somehow my she-penis stayed erect.

I felt my sphincter pulsate around the butt plug.

Where was Grady? Had he forgotten about me? Could he guarantee my safety? Did he even care about it? Did he care about me?

I was locked in like a lamb waiting for slaughter.

I felt I was losing all track of time. Perhaps it was getting dark outside. Had I missed breakfast, lunch and dinner?

My energy levels were so low.

What if I passed out due to low blood sugar or low blood pressure? Was there anywhere safe in here to safely sit down? I was so concerned at the potential for injury with the sex toy stuffed deep inside my ass.

I thought I heard someone whistle.

I listened.

I concentrated.

I eliminated the least likely.

It was just the wind of the storm, my only source of company.

I pressed the back of one hand over my ass. Grady's cum had long since dried into my skin. But how long?

Was it possible he'd lay down for a rest and fallen asleep?

What if I was left here until morning?

I was *so* hungry, and my frantic worrying was only intensifying each weary sensation inside.

My pulse leapt as a heavy gust slammed rain against the window. For a split-second, I thought someone outside was doing something.

I had to get off my feet. I couldn't stand any longer. I carefully felt around the floor with my stilettos. They were so different to men's shoes, I'd no muscle memory to rely on.

The floor seemed relatively clear beneath me. There were what felt like some cables, but nothing too tricky to manoeuvre myself upon.

I slowly lowered myself to one knee, and the butt plug inside played happy havoc with the changing shape of my rectum.

The gag muted my whines.

I sucked for air, then gradually brought down the other knee, easing the tension inside.

My erection still refused to relent.

I gently eased my ass downwards, panting through the gag as I imagined the possible pain striking an unseen item could cause.

The cold ground grazed my cheeks.

My sphincter involuntarily tightened on the toy.

I grimaced.

Fuck pig.

I tried to move my knees into a cross-legged position, propping my body weight on my penetrated anus.

"Mmmmmmpppppphhhhhh," I bleated.

Agony peaked.

I dragged air to my lungs, inflating my chest and sucking in my stomach, and used the cuffed heels of my hands to give myself added support.

Pain slowly subsided.

I tucked my legs under each other, the heels of each shoe sticking out to the sides.

I gradually caught my breath.

My clit needed orgasm, as if the rigorous punishment within and of being stripped, cuffed, gagged and hooded only drove my sensuality deeper. I felt humiliated, yet humbled. I'd learnt my lesson. Grady would not have to fear me snooping through his belongings again. I'd respect both him and his home until the moment I was free to leave.

The storm outside grew louder. I reasoned it had to be sometime in the evening.

Why hadn't he come back? I was so sorry. *So* sorry!

Chills overwhelmed my body from underneath. How long could I stay on the ground before the coldness became a threat to my well-being? How could I even stand again? It'd be too dangerous to my rear. I could damage it.

And I really didn't want to damage it.

I wanted to preserve it, predominantly so I could present it to him.

I wondered if he'd call it an ass... Or a pussy. Perhaps even my she-pussy.

My she-cock throbbed.

I heard whistling again.

It wasn't my imagination, nor was it the wind.

The key turned in the lock.

My pulse went into overdrive.

The door was opened.

I sat in terrified silence, wondering if it was someone else.

They didn't move. They didn't speak. They just, I guessed, watched.

My legs were spread at my thighs, then curved at my knees and one calf was crossed under the other, completely exposing my erection.

They moved into the shed, leaving the door open behind them.

I mumbled to no avail under the potato sack.

Rough, manly fingers took to my chest, tweaking each nipple in turn.

My instinct said it was Grady. I wanted it to be. It had to be.

I tilted my head back, begging him with my body language to unmask me.

His fingers moved from my nipples. They grabbed hold of the potato sack.

I swallowed.

The sack was hauled off my head.

CHAPTER 18

I stared up at him, blinking as my eyes adjusted to the light.

He looked down at me, breathing heavily. Had he been doing work? Heavy lifting perhaps? His hair was wet – outdoor work in the storm? – and sexy as hell.

I was shocked when I realised, and made a muffled attempt at speech.

He grinned, as if enjoying the sight of me squirm.

My clit leaked a tiny spec of juice.

He pushed my head forward, then unfastened the ball gag and pulled it free from my mouth. "Are you okay, fuck pig?"

My heart was pounding. "Outside," I squealed.

The wind blew the shed door shut.

"I can see daylight. I thought it was night time. I thought you'd locked me in here all day, Grady!"

He adjusted his crotch in his jeans, as he laughed at me. "Don't be silly, Maxine." He was looking past my head to my sex. "It wouldn't be safe to leave you in the cock ring for more than thirty minutes."

What? That couldn't be right. I'd been in here for hours! Surely. But my senses. It couldn't really have been just... "Half an hour?"

He reached down and aggressively pulled the ring from my clit. "That's right, gorgeous, it's just after midday. Lunchtime, in fact."

I felt the hint at my feminine role in the home.

"Did you learn your lesson?" he demanded.

"Yes, Grady. I'll never do anything like that again."

"Ever?"

I gulped, realising only too much how that implied I'd be here longer than the rest of the day. "Yes, Grady. Of course. I'll *never* anger you like that again. And I won't follow you or mention your... Y'know who."

He stroked his fingers through my hair. "You're a good girl, Maxine."

"Thank you," I whispered. "Has it *really* only been thirty minutes?"

"Yes." He ran his muddied fingers down my forehead to my

cheeks, dirtying my face like my knees. He brought them to my lips. "Kiss them."

I hesitated.

"Do you want to go through your punishment again..."

But they were filthy!

"Fuck pig?"

I quickly puckered up and laid my lips lovingly on his digits, kissing them one-by-one as he turned them over.

"That's nice, Maxine. You're a good girl at heart."

I slipped more of my mouth over his big middle finger, tasting the dirt of the earth.

"Would you like to go back to the cottage now?" he asked, reaching his hands down and taking hold of my arms.

"Please, Grady. I'm so cold."

He pulled me to my feet. "You deserve a reward for being so sexy and dignified in your punishment, don't you?"

My anus contracted around the butt plug. "Are you going to take my cuffs off-"

"And, look, you're covered in mud." Grady lifted me off my heels. "You're so filthy." He threw me over his shoulder, then spun around. "You deserve a shower." He pushed the shed door open and carried me naked out into the storm.

CHAPTER 19

"Grady," I screamed, rattling my cuffs above my rear in mid-air, "please don't drop me!"

He swatted my ass, the stings reverberating the walls of my anus against the sex toy, then he turned to unlock the front door.

I frantically looked at my surroundings, trying to see if there was any sign of a main road – there wasn't – or of the person who'd looked in the bedroom – there wasn't – or any indication of a world away from Grady at all... There wasn't.

He carried me into the cottage.

Rainwater trickled down my naked body.

Grady stared lustfully at me, as he set me down on my stilettos in the living room.

I grimaced as I found my feet. "You forgot to uncuff me," I protested.

"No, I didn't."

I sighed. "Well, Grady, you certainly forgot to take the butt plug out of me."

He smiled.

"You didn't?"

He shook his head.

My erection coursed straight up, striking an oddly effeminate pose.

"If you could see yourself right now, baby," he said. "Your make-up's a mess, your legs are covered in muck..." He grabbed me by my arm, and half-turned me away from him. "Your ass's saturated in spunk."

My heart skipped a beat.

"I'm going to shower you, Maxine."

"*You're* going to shower me, Grady?"

He nodded.

But I was perfectly capable of showering myself. "Okay." I smiled. "I guess I'm okay with that."

I really missed having access to my mobile phone. I couldn't even remember where I'd left it in the cottage. It left me feeling totally isolated from the world..

Grady took my sexy heels from me and set them neatly under the bathroom sink. Then he took a final glance at my vulnerable and dirty nakedness. "Ready?"

"Yes, Grady."

He turned the tap, sending cold water over my body.

I squealed aloud.

"It's just an old country system, sweet cheeks," he insisted, aiming the shower head over me as I cowered. "It'll get warm in a minute."

Freezing water, even worse than the rain outside, soaked my skin. "Please point it away!"

"No."

More washed over me, as the mud began to run down my legs.

"Turn around, sissy!"

I twisted away from him.

"Stick your ass out!"

I jutted out my rear.

Grady fired the water over me.

I was so thankful when the water turned warm, then hot in a matter of seconds.

His dried cum ran down the crack of my ass, to my scrotum, then my thighs to the puddle of mud beneath my feet, pooling around the sinkhole.

"Goodbye cum," I said. "Till we meet again."

Grady aimed the hot jets over my back, as I stretched out my arms, relishing the beautiful warmth.

When I eventually turned around, his eyes were drawn to my erect she-penis.

"Are you sexually frustrated, Maxine?"

"Yes, Grady," I said, wishing he'd take hold of her and massage her to orgasm.

"Those cuffs frustrating you?"

I shook my head defiantly.

"No?"

"I'd *gladly* stay in these handcuffs for the rest of my stay here, if I knew it brought you joy, Grady."

His eyes narrowed. "Are you a sycophant, Max?"

I swallowed. *Not Maxine*? "What does that mean?" I asked.

"You tell me what I want to hear?"

My erection fluttered under the full rush of the water. "I guess so, Grady."

"But in order to gain an advantage over me?"

I shook my head. "No, sir, to please you! Only to please you! To serve you!"

He switched off the water.

I flinched as he brought his hand to me.

"Relax, buttercup, I'm not going to hurt you." He brushed his fingers over my flat tummy. "You're a beautiful, young lady."

Not a sissy?

"So refined."

Not a slut?

"So deserving of this," he said, and took a gentle yet manly hold of my sex. "This is as pretty a clit as I've seen on any DVD from around the world, Maxine."

I felt the cuffs dig into my wrists.

Grady ever so slowly rolled my foreskin back with his fingers.

Shyness overwhelmed me as my slit slipped into view.

He sheathed it again, rolling my foreskin forward. "Do you like men touching you down there?"

I reluctantly nodded.

"Do you like *me* touching you down there?"

"I love it," I said, and met his second stroke with a slow one of my own.

"May I?" he asked.

I desperately wanted him to masturbate me, and nodded profusely.

Grady lowered himself to his knees at the edge of the shower, then he slid his face forward and opened his mouth, taking my sex inside.

"Oh my God!" I hadn't expected that at all!

He sucked on my little thing.

"Wow!"

Grady grunted, then took me all the way to my base, nesting his nostrils in my landing strip.

I panted.

He licked all around my length.

My knees almost buckled.

Grady led his tongue to the tip, then took his mouth away.

My sphincter tightened on the toy. "Please don't stop, Grady. Please. I need release."

He just grinned.

I groaned. "You enjoy teasing me?"

"I enjoy *torturing* you, Maxine." He reached his hand between my legs and cupped my balls. "You do feel very tense." He slid his hand further behind, pressing his fingers against the butt plug into my ass. "Does that help?"

I was catching my breath. "No- No... But it's nice."

Grady pressed harder. "Some shemales can cum simply by anal stimulation."

I felt dizzy. It had to be impossible. No one could-

He hit the base of the toy.

I gasped.

"You're going to learn how, Maxine."

What? No?

"I promise."

Now? How? I couldn't-

"But not yet."

I wheezed.

Grady pulled his hand away, then switched the shower back on. "But first I'm going to finish cleaning that shit off your body." He sprayed my face before I could shut my mouth or my eyes. "Then I'm going to uncuff you. And no, before you ask, you cannot masturbate. I forbid you to cum without my permission, and even then it'll be solely through what your asshole can take."

I felt so uncomfortable at the prospect.

"When I take your cuffs off, baby, it's so you can put your make-up on again."

I was grateful for the smallest of mercies.

"Then you're to present yourself for inspection in the bedroom." Inspection?

"*If* you pass, you can put on another outfit I've brought down for you. But if you *don't* pass inspection..."

What? What would happen?

CHAPTER 20

I walked out of the bathroom with my towel covering my body from my chest to my crotch, just as a woman would cover her breasts and her vagina.

Grady was stood with his arms folded in the doorway to the bedroom.

I lowered my eyes when I saw the stern look on his face. Was there something wrong with my make-up? I thought I'd done at least as good a job as before.

"Did you cum?" he demanded. "How many times?"

"I didn't!" I hadn't.

He grabbed my towel and hauled it away.

My clit was still erect.

"Good girl." He smiled as he gazed at my sex. "I was afraid you'd masturbate her."

"You were *afraid-*"

"For you, Maxine." Grady stepped to one side, and gestured for me to the enter the bedroom. "For what I'd have to do you if you failed to follow my orders."

My ass was swatted as I passed him, stinging me both outside and in.

"Stand next to the bed."

I obeyed him.

He stared at me.

"Is something wrong, Grady?"

He ignored me.

My stomach rumbled.

"Are you hungry, Maxine?"

I reluctantly nodded, fearful he'd use it as an excuse to punish me again.

"We can't have that. You can cook us both lunch after."

After? After what?

He walked right up to me until his crotch – albeit clothed – came into contact with mine. "Have you really never had an orgasm without being touched there?"

"Never," I said.

He grinned. "I'll fuck the cum out of you."

I gasped. What? How? When? Was this the event which would precede lunch?

His eyes roamed my face.

"Is my make-up okay?" I asked.

"Perfect, Maxine. You look like an angel. *My* angel." He took my face in his hands and brought my lips to his.

I felt electricity surge through my body as I shared a gentle kiss with this hulk of a man.

He used his lips to part mine, then slipped his tongue inside.

My clit buzzed against his groin and my sphincter tightened on the sex toy.

Grady passionately twirled my tongue around his, easily exercising his dominant masculinity.

I dared put my hands on his torso.

He kissed me faster.

I wanted him more, and began to undo the buttons on his shirt.

He pulled my hands away.

I groaned.

He belayed my protests with his superior technique.

I was breathless. Had I *ever* been kissed like this?

Grady's fingers strayed to my waist, then around my hips to my buttocks. He dug his fingertips into my flesh as he sucked my tongue into his mouth.

I moaned.

He pressed the base of the toy deeper into my anus.

I wanted to pull his cock out from his jeans. I wanted it in my hands, on my clit, in my mouth and even to replace that plug in my rear.

Grady took hold of the base, then carefully guided it out from my ass.

I accidentally broke the kiss, as I was fighting for breath.

"You okay?" he asked.

I nodded, and looked down in time to see precum from my clit leak onto his jeans.

"Did you enjoy that?" He brought the toy all the way out.

"It was amazing, Grady." I looked lustfully into his eyes. "Kiss me again."

He shook his head. "I only wanted to kiss you while you still tasted good." He held up the butt plug. "Clean this... With your mouth."

What?

"Knock that look off your face, Maxine. I'm sure you've done this before. And worse."

I had, but with someone I'd been in a relationship with. Someone I'd once thought I loved.

Grady took hold of my clit. He gently massaged her. "You like that?"

"Yes," I wheezed.

"I won't stop if you start sucking your ass off this." He pointed the part which had been inside me at my mouth. "Go on." He pushed it against my lips.

I parted them.

Grady shoved it all the way inside me, then started to tug on my sex.

I could taste my asshole. Unmistakeably. But the sensations in my clit were too wonderful to be shy. I tongued what'd probed my hole, almost lovingly licking off my innards.

Grady masturbated me more furiously.

I really began to give head to the butt plug, and flicked my eyes to his.

He was watching me.

I deliberately made amorous noises as I sucked.

"You were born to be a girl, Maxine, weren't you?"

I parted my lips. "Yes," I struggled, then slammed them shut and sucked on the sex toy.

He pumped my sex. "Nearly done?"

I vigorously shook my head, then ploughed my mouth to the very base of the toy, plucking it from his fingers.

He felt my balls with his free hand. "You're trying to make this last. You're hoping I'll help you empty these... I won't." Yet he continued to pummel my she-penis.

I swallowed the taste of my asshole.

"Good girl, gulp it all down."

I tried desperately not to gag, despite the despicable remnants I felt falling down my throat.

"I bet your ass pussy is delicious."

I humped his hand.

He squeezed my balls.

I grimaced.

"Sorry," he said, grinning.

I raised my head, eyeing the ceiling, and let the plug fall, filling my mouth.

He slid his fingers from my scrotum, along the little path of my perineum, to the edge of my anus. "I love no panty day, Maxine."

I felt myself nearing the point of no return.

"You want so badly to spray your clit juice, don't you?"

I sucked so loudly.

He pressed his middle finger into my hole. "*Don't* you?"

I kept my head up, but surrendered a nod.

"Desperately?" Grady penetrated me all the way to his knuckle.

I whimpered.

He gave a slight laugh.

I lowered my chin, holding the toy with my teeth.

He locked eyes with me.

Would he finger-fuck me to orgasm? I even nodded to him.

Grady slipped a second finger inside. "You're so open. Are you normally so open?"

It'd been the sex toy. I shook my head, not wanting him to think I was some kind of sex-mad cock slut.

He laughed. "I believe you... Thousands wouldn't."

I felt fantastic within his touch, then tasted just too much of my anus from the toy, and coughed, dropping it to the bedroom floor.

Grady stilled on my sex.

"Please don't stop."

He squeezed so hard, until more precum dripped out.

"I know how to control my sluts, Maxine."

I panted, bending my back to try to take more of his fingers.

"The trick's always to leave them wanting more."

"How?" I cried. "How do you know?"

He pulled his fingers free from my ass.

I was reduced to stamping my feet.

"I'll tell you," he said, smiling widely. "You've told me a little about yourself, it's only right I tell you a little about my past before... Before I *fuck* you."

I gulped.

"But over lunch. I want you to get dressed first."

I hesitated. "In what, Grady?" There was nothing left out for me.

"You choose." He pointed behind the bed. "I brought some things for you to pick from. They're beside your side."

My side? He made it sound like this was a permanent fixture.

"Some jewellery too." He ran the back of his fingers down my cheeks. "But under no circumstances are you to wear any panties, okay?"

"Yes, Grady. It's no panty day."

"Oh, angel, how I'm going to love you. You're a born subordinate."

CHAPTER 21

Subordinate. Born subordinate. Those words – that phrase – circled my every thought, as I set Grady's lunch down before him.

"May I?" I said, holding salt over his plate.

He snatched it from me. "You'd never give me enough, Maxine."

I gazed at him, wondering when he'd give me more of *his* salt.

He eyed me in my new outfit and jewellery. "A pearl necklace, baby? I sincerely hope you're dropping a hint with that one."

"Whatever could you mean, Grady?"

He took his first bite.

I waited for his opinion before I dared start mine.

"Good," he said.

I began eating.

"Stop."

I froze.

He gestured to the chair at the head of the table, right next to him. "I don't want you sitting opposite me, Maxine. What's the point in no panty day, if I can't see your clit? Move here."

"Yes, sir."

He watched me sit. "Spread your legs." He grinned. "That's better." He chewed. "She's *so* small."

I felt my face redden.

"It's a complement."

"You were going to tell me something about yourself, Grady?"

"Indeed, baby. About my past. I'm sure you're interested... Are you scared?"

"A little," I reluctantly admitted, even though it was still actually quite a lot.

"You should be. I've a dark past."

My clit half-stiffened.

"You might want to walk out that door right now, while you still have a chance."

Was he serious?

Grady chewed on pastry and beef.

"But... The storm?" And my male clothes-

He slammed down his knife and fork, then grabbed my clit. "I can't keep my hands off her, Maxine. I'm obsessed with your little sex. You don't seriously believe you're the first city slut I've had out here at the cottage, do you? No, you know better. You can sense the shemale sex palace this place has been."

I groaned.

"But I bet you want to know how."

I nodded, as he released my she-rod and went back to his lunch.

"With no phone and no internet, seemingly in the middle-of-nowhere."

Seemingly?

"Maxine, it's simple... I didn't do it alone."

What? Who? I felt fear throb within the confines of my sexy knee-high boots.

"I had an accomplice."

My clit bobbed up.

"Or, what I should say, baby, is... I *have* an accomplice."

I froze. "The person I saw outside?"

Grady touched my leg. "If I now forbid you to leave, what're you going to do, Maxine? If I tell you that if you try to run now, I'll catch you, I'll tie you up and I'll do things to you you never thought possible, just what would you do..."

I gulped.

"Slut?"

CHAPTER 22

My wrists were bound behind the back of the chair.

Grady pulled my hair until my neck was cranked back over the top of the chair. He slipped his tongue into my mouth again.

My clit throbbed under my short denim skirt, despite my trepidation, and I hungrily kissed him back.

He fondled my tits through my see-through top.

I fed more of my tongue to him.

He let go of my hair.

I couldn't lose more of his trust, and tried to steal more from his kiss.

Grady shoved my head forward, then sat down and started to eat again. "There's another man with similar tastes to mine in the local community."

There was a community? Somewhere I could escape to for help?

"Don't ask how we discovered each other's tastes, it doesn't matter. Only know that many a shemale whore has provided for them... For both of us."

My stomach rumbled.

"You shouldn't have tried to run, Maxine."

"I was role-playing, Grady. I thought you'd know."

"Shut up. Don't insult my intelligence." He pushed his plate to one side, then lifted mine. "I won't let this go to waste."

I was *so* hungry, and I'd been so keen to please him I'd barely taken a couple of bites before I'd stupidly tried to run.

"His name's Dominic."

"Was that the man I saw at the window?"

"No," Grady snapped.

But it had to be!

"You *didn't* see anyone at the window, Maxine, understand?"

No, I really did. But. What if? "Yes, Grady," I said, and looked down at my clit. "It was my stupid whore's imagination."

Grady laughed.

"Am I going to meet Dominic? I mean, are you going to make me?"

"He used to go different cities, pick-up transsexuals and bring them back here. Some of them were really average, barely passable. I don't go for the unremarkable, Maxine, you can attest to that. But when Dominic did bring a slut I was attracted to..." He was smiling as he chewed. "I'd show them the way we do things out here in the country. Yes, we've got manners. But we leave our pleases and thank yous at the door when sex like that's on the cards."

I gulped.

"I'd one chained up in my bed one night, face down, and I fucked and fucked her asshole until she came hard on the duvet without having her clit touched even once."

I shuddered.

"Then I walked naked out through the living room where Dominic's slut was sucking him off as he drank a bottle of whiskey. I grabbed her and pulled her away. He tried to protest, but he was falling asleep. He was out for the count before I'd even got her outdoors."

"Outdoors?" I asked.

Grady laughed again. "I dragged her out to the shed, Maxine. Oh fuck, I chained her up as well and then I piled every inch of my cock into her tiny, teeny hole. She was saying it was her first time, and it so obviously was... I enjoyed taking her virginity... It was like I was leaving her with a lifetime of doubt about her sexuality."

"What do you mean... Doubt?"

He studied a piece of meat on his fork. "She didn't enjoy it."

I found hope in the most despicable of spots in his story. "You mean she didn't cum?"

"Of course she came, Maxine. I make all these shemale sluts cum. And yes, without being touched between their legs."

I blushed, knowing I was inadequate.

"None were as pretty nor as angelic as you, Maxine... I promise."

It didn't matter even if it was the truth. I'd never be able to climax without having my clit stimulated. It was impossible.

"It's almost like my cock's built just perfectly to hit the prostate gland and give those incredible orgasms."

I was stunned.

Grady put his hand on my leg. "You're an angel, Maxine... May I call you angel?"

I nodded, as he slid his hand closer to my clit.

"Oh, just look at that landing strip. You're a devil in angel's clothing," he added, then eyed my erect nipples poking through my sheer white top.

I knew what I had to do, as Grady reached into the top pocket of his shirt. "Fuck me, Grady," I pleaded, straining my bound wrists. "Fuck me like the whore I am."

He laughed, then set down a sheet of paper. "These are your chores."

I leaned forward and saw a long, long list.

Grady tapped his forefinger on the page. "You carry these out..."

Some of them were outdoors!

"*Then* we can have some fun."

CHAPTER 23

I was almost glad to get a break from Grady when the last of my chores took me out of the cottage and to a barn on the far side of the property. He'd fondled my breasts, my belly, my legs and, of course, my clit as I'd cleaned every single room. He'd even made me wet his fingers before he'd put them up inside me as I bent over on all fours to scrub the kitchen floor.

"Mopping won't suffice," he'd insisted.

Almost glad, as the brute force of the storm blew my clit back between my legs and froze my nipples to the point where I was afraid they'd slice open my top.

I was terrified of being seen by Dominic, as I skipped quickly towards the barn. Whereabouts did he live? Was he close? Could he see me without me seeing him? I felt so vulnerable, and wished for the worst of the storm to pass by evening.

I struggled to unbolt the barn door, as my skirt blew up over my ass. I cursed no panty day.

Rain bounced off the door and splashed my face.

I sighed. There was my make-up ruined *again*.

I got inside, and shook myself dry.

The stench of the barn was almost as painstaking as the physical labour. I seriously wondered when Grady had last cleaned the place.

The door creaked.

My eyes darted.

It was just the wind.

But what if Dominic did turn up? How many favours did Grady owe him for all the *city shemale sluts* he'd provided him down the years?

I was adamant I wouldn't be a whore pawn in their games.

Oh, angel, how I'm going to love you. You're a born subordinate.

I returned to my chores, hosing down the outside of the pig pen.

Fuck pig.

I stopped hosing suddenly, certain I'd heard someone else in the barn.

"Hello?" I called.

No answer.

"Grady, is that you?"

The wind whipped at the wooden walls.

I looked up to the roof, and wondered if it was secure at the best of times never mind in this extreme weather. It creaked.

I started to apply pressure on the handle of the hose again-

A shadow cast in the corner of my eye.

I shot a glance.

There was nothing there.

"Dominic?" I dared ask, my feet ready to spin on my stilettos and take me off into the early evening.

Silence but for the elements outside.

I was cold and becoming both increasingly agitated. I sprayed water on the outside wall of the pen again.

Hands grabbed me to either side.

I screamed, and dropped the hose on the ground.

The fingers tightened.

"Let me go!" I squealed.

He turned me around.

"I hate you!"

He grinned. "No, you don't."

I noticed how he'd changed his shirt. It was really, really sexy.

"You approve then, angel?"

"Yes, Grady, but *don't* sneak up on me like that again. I was scared. I thought you were-"

"Dominic," he interrupted. "Yes, I heard you calling out for him."

I slapped his chest. "In fear of him!"

"Yeah, yeah." He released his grip on me, then looked me up and down. "Mmmmmm, hard work looks well on you, Maxine."

I was chilled right through my flesh to my bone. "Well, it doesn't feel well on me."

"I'll take care of the heavy lifting." He gestured to pallets in the corner. "A sexy sissy like you should conserve your muscle, not build it."

I agreed.

Grady looked down, to the edge of my short skirt where part of my clit was just visible. "Tell me something, baby, have you always been cock-hungry?"

I sighed.

"No, no. I mean, you just look so hot stood like that."

I had mud on my hands, arms and legs. Perhaps on my face too. I felt anything but hot-

Grady took hold of my sex again.

I moaned aloud as he rubbed her.

"You like that?" he demanded.

"Yes, sir."

"You like your clit being massaged, angel?"

"I like it being masturbated, sir."

He cleared his throat. "Were you really going to run away when I told you about Dominic?"

I shook my head.

"You *were* playing?"

"Yes."

"I was playing too, when I tied you up with that tie. That's why it wasn't tight."

It had been tight. "I'm not playing when I say my fear of Dominic is real, Grady."

He covered my whole clit with less than half his hand.

"I don't want to meet him."

"Okay, angel." He reached to gently rub my arm. "So you *do* really want to be here?"

I took a deep breath. "Yes," I said finally, and I didn't feel like I was lying. At least, not entirely. I had concerns. I only felt safe in his arms. Truly safe. And that counted for something.

"And if I asked you to give me a blowjob right here, right now... What would you say, angel?"

I looked to one side of the barn, then the other.

The storm battered the huge, heavy door.

I dropped my bare knees to the cold, wet, muddy cement ground. Instinct told me he'd tell me to stop when I proved how far I'd go, then he'd take me back to the cottage to do it properly in the warm.

Grady looked down.

I smiled up, then unbuttoned his jeans.

His huge cock was visible underneath.

"I love no panty day," I said, then dragged his jeans down to his knees and feasted my nostrils on the whiff of his manliness.

"Me too, angel."

I hesitated. What? He was really going to let me do this here? Now?

"Suck it, Maxine."

I wrapped my fingers around his girth, and shivered.

"The size intimidates you?"

The fierce coldness did. "Sorry, sir."

"Is it the biggest you've ever seen?"

No. "Yes, Grady." But it was about to be the biggest I'd ever... I stuffed it between my lips.

"Fuck."

I slammed his shaft against the back of my throat.

"Oh, angel, that's incredible."

I slurped.

"*You're* incredible."

I was no virgin.

Grady lost his voice.

I lost my lips in the base of his cock. His scent was wonderful. His texture divine. And his taste to absolutely die for. It'd been too long since I'd had one of these in my mouth. I licked the underside of his girth with such devotion my attention was almost permanently diverted from the coldness against my knees.

Grady's lower abdomen appeared to tremble in front of my eyes.

I deliberately bent his cock first to my left, then to my right.

"Easy, girl," he whispered, then pulled it out.

I breathed in, ignoring the trail of saliva which led from my lips to his rod.

He slapped his cock against my face.

I was stunned. Not at the strength of the strike. It was gentle. But I thought I deserved more appreciation.

He did it again, then wiped saliva on me. "Oh, Maxine, let me wash your dirty, laboured skin with my shaft."

I let him.

Grady shoved it back inside.

I wet it all over.

He pulled it out, slapped the other side of my face, then wiped my saliva over my cheek.

"Thank you, Grady," I said, as my clit ached with hardness.

"Oh no, honey, the thanks are all mine. You're so beautiful." He held his cock in front of my lips. "May I?"

I didn't answer. I didn't nod. I simply parted my lips and lay my eyes on it.

He slid it into my mouth again.

I twisted my tongue around it, then slammed forward, taking it all. As I withdrew to the tip, I sucked up all my saliva and the dirty remnants of my afternoon's work he'd just washed off my face. I'd never have been into such filth with anyone else, but with Grady I just couldn't resist.

He groaned.

I sucked fast to his base, then back again, placing my palms on his hips to hold him where I wanted.

"You're so good at this," he mumbled. "I can tell you've had practice."

I let his length fall, and felt his flesh immediately tense under my fingers. I dared look up to him. "So have you."

His gaze back gave nothing away.

I closed my eyes and took his behemoth back down to my throat.

Wind caused every corner of the barn to creak.

I concentrated only on the cock in my crevice, gargling around it, then swallowing the mixture of saliva and precum. Precum wouldn't suffice, though. I needed to drain his balls again. I'd felt his warm semen on my ass, now I wanted it in my belly. I devoured his dick, using every piece of expertise my experience had taught me.

Grady slipped his thumbs between my palms and his hips, then started to drill himself forward, meeting my lustful strokes.

I smiled around his giant girth.

"You gonna swallow?" he asked.

I ignored the stupid question.

"Are you, angel?"

I lifted my eyes to his, sucked him harder, and hoped he understood.

Grady grunted as he powered his cock forward, slamming his big balls against my smooth chin.

I reached down and hauled my skirt to my waist. What was the point in no panty day if I couldn't give my man a good view?

"Don't touch her," he said.

I moved my hands behind my back, knowing how much he enjoyed binding my wrists there, and plunged my mouth to his base.

Grady tried to fuck my face.

I planted my lips around his base, like a soft, living cock ring.

He tried in vain to fuck my resistance.

I gagged.

His balls tensed.

I adapted my airway to hold his throbbing member in place.

"This is insane!" he cried.

My heart sang... This guy thought making a city slut cum without touching her was something? Ha!

Grady vigorously pumped the tiniest of spaces my mouth allowed him between his base and the back of my throat.

I tried to swallow his shaft.

"Jesus!"

Literally.

"Oh God, angel!"

I felt him smash my throat.

Grady erupted hard.

I clenched with everything but my incisors, desperate to sweep up every ounce of his load.

His balls emptied between my lips.

I gulped hard and fast.

His shaft tore my lips from his base.

My squeals were instantaneously silenced as he grabbed the back of my head.

I felt his seed slip down inside to my stomach.

Grady held me in place as he violently fucked the rest of his orgasm into my face.

CHAPTER 24

I could hear dripping, and diligently sucked from the corners of my mouth, refusing to waste any of his sperm. Then I realised. I hadn't spilled a drop. The dripping was the sound of a leak from the roof. Rainwater was getting in. I sucked in my cheeks regardless, then swallowed.

Grady hauled up his jeans.

"Was that everything you hoped it'd be?" I asked.

He didn't answer me.

I'd experienced alpha male guilt all too often after they climaxed, but I wouldn't accept it from Grady. I reached my hand out to his.

He paused, then looked at my fingers on his. "It was... Fantastic."

"Good. Does that mean I can get off the cold ground now?"

His eyes were still on my fingers.

"Grady?"

He shook his head and exhaled. "This reminds me of when I was in Africa, many years ago." He pulled out a cigarette and lit it. "You wouldn't have believed the weather compared to what we have here today. The heat was staggering, Maxine. It was dangerous to be exposed to direct sunlight. You couldn't go anywhere without a supply of water, and if you did you made sure you'd plenty of bottled water with you."

Me on my cold knees reminded him of that?

"We were on a safari, a group of us all in our early twenties. One day we discovered an injured lion. Or so we thought. We decided we couldn't just leave it there to suffer."

I felt a pang of panic inside.

"Something had to be done."

I started to withdraw my fingers from his hand.

He turned his over to catch hold of mine. "But the lion had only lured us in with her cunning. She'd feigned her distress, her injury. To look at her, she appeared beautiful and vulnerable. It was decent human instinct which made us try to help."

My clit was soft.

"No one was killed, but two of us were injured. One badly. Permanently. He's never walked right again."

I silently breathed in.

"I learnt a lesson that day, Maxine."

What'd happened to Angel?

"A lesson I seemed to forget."

I anxiously breathed out.

"Someone who feigns weakness then demonstrates skill is to be doubted."

"Grady, I wasn't pretending to be unconscious when you found me-"

"I know," he snapped.

"You don't have to doubt me."

He stared down at me.

"May I get up, please?" I begged.

Grady brought me to my feet.

"Thank you." I fixed my skirt into a more ladylike, albeit short, fashion.

"You may not have pretended to be injured, but you have tried to act innocent, Maxine. The blowjob you just gave me proves you're anything but."

I'd never pretended to be innocent. "My past is my past, Grady. I just choose not to broadcast it. Please respect that."

"Who were you out here to meet?" he demanded.

I rolled my eyes. "Not this again."

He slid his hands to my elbows. "Yes, *this* again. I want to know who."

"No, Grady, it wouldn't be fair to say."

"But I *have* to know who was going to use you, Max-"

I cut my arms free from his grip. "It's Max*ine*," I stressed. "Don't use your jealousy as an excuse to try to hurt me now."

"Do you know his name?"

I felt my anger rising and gritted my teeth to control it. "Yes, Grady, and it's none of your business."

"Was it Dominic?"

My jaw dropped. "You think I was out here to be a girl for some other guy?"

"You have a landing strip."

"Because *I* like it, Grady!"

He rubbed his temples. "Was it Dominic?"

"You're crazy."

"Answer me."

I stepped back and folded my arms. I almost regretted the taste of his sperm still lingering on my tongue.

"Why won't you say yes or no?"

"Because it's stupid, Grady. If I thought I was meeting Dominic, why would I've been so afraid when I saw him at the window-"

"There wasn't anyone at the window, Maxine!"

The barn creaked.

I fixed my hair behind my ears. "This really isn't any of your business, Grady, but just so you know, no, I wasn't meeting Dominic." I wiped moisture from my face.

"But it probably *is* someone I know."

I reluctantly nodded.

"The community around here is small, tight-knit."

I was so cold.

"Did you give him your name?"

I looked away, regret beginning to fill my eyes with water. "I told him what I'd be driving."

"The pink fuck mobile," Grady said. "He may have seen it abandoned on the road... *Who* was it?"

"Don't make me say."

"Give me his name, Maxine."

"Please, Grady."

"Now."

I wiped my tears. "Is this what I have to look forward to?"

"I order you to."

"Really, Grady? A life of you walking over my every wish, my every desire."

"I *opened* you to your desires, Maxine. You'll thank me someday. Now, tell me his name... Before I lose my patience."

I looked to the wet ground. "He only told me his first name."

Grady went to speak.

"Nick," I said, and my insides felt hollow. I'd done something no one should ever do, betraying everything I'd ever believed in. I'd potentially outed an innocent man. "You can't say any-"

"I need to take off", Grady said, turning swiftly away from me.

"What? Where?" I started after him. "Back to the cottage?"

"Out."

I grabbed his arm.

He shrugged me away.

"Grady, please tell me where you're going-"

"It doesn't matter."

I hoped he was just going to storm off to his mother's in a fit of jealousy.

He stopped suddenly, then looked over his shoulder at me. "It's none of your business."

"Do you know him?" I asked.

He stared at me.

"Do you know Nick?"

"I won't be long."

"The storm, Grady, please be careful."

He mustered a semi-smile. "I think you *do* like me, Maxine."

"Of course I do, Grady. I really like you. Stay with me, please. Whatever you're planning, forget about it. I don't even know what Nick looks like. I don't care. I didn't know you until this weekend. I don't want him. I don't want *anyone* else. I just want to be your Maxine... Your angel."

Grady reached into his pocket, producing both his cigarettes and a key. "Get yourself back to the cottage." He gestured to my face. "Wash yourself, you're dirty."

I sighed, knowing in my heart he was going to pay Nick a visit and there wasn't anything I could say to change his mind.

"Fix your make-up, make yourself presentable..."

Presentable? Something in his tone drew my suspicions.

"Cook a feast."

A feast? "Grady?"

"What?" he asked, placing the key in my palm.

"We aren't expecting any visitors, are we?"

He turned, then walked out of the barn and into the storm without answering.

CHAPTER 25

My stomach performed a concerto of epic, hungry proportions as I made dinner for Grady and I, and I sincerely hoped it was just for the two of us.

The storm was fading outside, although it was still raining. If I had to escape, it was no longer impossible.

I tested the pie I was preparing, slightly burning the tip of my tongue, but I was so glad to get food down. It tasted pretty good too.

Night had fallen, and he still wasn't home.

I was worried. And I actually missed him. What if he didn't come back? What if this Nick guy and him had got into a fight? All it'd take would be one fatal blow-

I told myself to shut up in my head, then fixed the thong-shaped rear of my swimsuit between my butt cheeks. Yes, after a long, hard-earned shower, I'd put my make-up back on, giving myself a real energetic look, and gone totally Baywatch when I found a sexy, red swimsuit. I didn't have the bust for it, but it was so tight around my ass I knew Grady would love it. I'd checked myself out in the mirror several times to be certain. And I was.

My stomach rumbled again.

Then there was more rumbling.

I looked hopefully up to the kitchen window and saw headlights. They were approaching the house.

I listened carefully.

It was Grady's tractor!

He dropped two sports bags by the door on the living room floor, then looked at me.

As the sweet smell of a home-cooked meal wafted over me, I placed my palms on the kitchen counter to reveal my tight waist and set my matching red stiletto heels far apart, rotating my rump for his eyes to feast on.

"What the fuck?" he demanded.

My heart pounded.

"Maxine?"

I wondered where he'd been. What he'd heard. And if Nick had shared with him our private conversation online that'd led me to the countryside?

Grady pointed at my hole. "Don't you know what day it is?"

"It's... Well, it's-"

"No fucking panty day." He came forward.

I turned my ass from him and backed away.

"So disrespectful," he said, and hauled out the kitchen drawer. "Stand there." He grabbed a pair of scissors. "Stay still!"

I froze.

"You thought you'd be Pamela Anderson, did you?"

I gulped.

Grady took hold of the narrow front of my swimsuit, stretching it out from my tiny clit. He kneeled down, shoving the scissors aggressively over the fabric, then snipped.

I winced, imagining pain in my sex.

He twirled me around.

I momentarily stumbled.

"You will respect no panty day until it's over, slut." He pulled the thong part out from between my cheeks, then cut it away.

I felt the fabric fall from between my legs.

Grady smacked my ass. "That's better." He rubbed my rear. "Such a fine arse." He forced my buttocks apart. "Such a fine she-pussy."

"Thank you, Grady," I whispered.

He turned me to him again.

My clit hung lifelessly in front of his face.

"Your front sex, just like your rear sex, deserves to be exposed."

My stomach rumbled.

"Is dinner nearly ready, angel?" he asked, his tone immediately friendly, as he stood up and took a seat at the table.

"Yes, sir. It's a meat pie, with all the sides I imagined you'd like. It's a feast. I'll serve it now."

He sat with his legs spread wide. "Good girl."

Grady armed moisture from his brow. "I'm getting the meat sweats now. This is fantastic. I can't remember the last time I tasted food this good."

I smiled. "So, are you going to tell me where you were?"

He licked pastry from his knife, then swallowed. "You must

really love dick, Max."

I wasn't going to rise to it.

"Why the swimsuit?"

I could be just as stubborn as him, and didn't answer.

Grady sighed. "Max*ine*?"

"I knew my ass would look great in it. If you didn't want me to wear it, why'd you leave it out for me?"

"I did want you to wear it, just not on no panty day."

I watched him add more salt to his dinner. "Sorry, Grady," I whispered, and instantly chastised myself for apologising.

He leaned to one side, then looked at my crotch. "You're not aroused."

"No."

He pointed his fork at me.

So rude!

"Angel, did you masturbate while I was out?"

"Absolutely not, Grady. You forbid me from doing that."

"That's right, I did, so why aren't you hard?"

I set my cutlery down, then crossed my legs to restore enough dignity to be taken seriously... In a red swimsuit in a cottage in the countryside. "I don't want to start an argument, so please hear my tone." I spoke with such effeminate gentleness. "You stormed off virtually the same second I told you Nick's name. I'm worried about what happened. Did you go see him? Do you even know him?"

"I know him," Grady said, before downing several carrots and a small potato in one mouthful.

I watched him for what felt like an eternity, waiting for him to offer more information without me having to feel like I was a wife from the 1950's forced to nag it out of him.

"Why are your legs crossed?"

I folded my arms.

He gave me a side-glance.

I opened my legs for him. "I know you took your tractor out, Grady. I saw you pull up in it."

He shrugged.

All I'd done was go online, find a seemingly nice guy to chat to, things had taken a turn towards a booty call – big deal – and now I was worried sick about the possible implications for his private life. "Did you go see him, Grady?"

He grinned.

"I know this is a small community." Most probably not as forward-thinking as the city I'd come from.

Grady set down his knife and fork. "You ask too many questions."

"Just tell me, *did* you go see Nick?"

"Maxine, that meal was truly delicious." He placed his palm on my bare knee. "But now I want to see how you compare."

I hesitated.

Grady stood, beginning to remove his jeans. "It's about time you got your reward."

I saw his huge cock again. "My reward?" Was he really going to fuck me with that?

"I'm going to make you cum, angel."

CHAPTER 26

"Just answer me one question first," he said. "Do you want this?" He gestured his thumb first to his chest, then to mine.

"Yes, Grady."

He pulled me suddenly to my feet.

My clit flopped to and fro.

He started to kiss me, first with just his lips, as he caressed my bare arms. Then his arms went around my back, he pulled me tight to him and his tongue slipped passionately into my mouth.

I melted into his masculinity, pulling at his shirt and returning his kiss with desire.

He held me so tight.

I rested my cooler arms on his warmer back.

His crotch was against mine.

I felt his hardness against my sex.

Grady explored the inner parts of my lower lip with his tongue.

I'd never had anyone do this to me, and it was amazing! Such an unexplored erogenous zone!

His hands moved to my rear, squeezing a buttock each.

I moaned against his mouth.

He pulled me by my ass tighter to his body.

My clit was coming to life against him.

He grunted.

I slipped my fingers around his waist, then lowered them towards his mammoth cock.

Grady made enough of a gap between us.

I didn't hesitate. I took hold of it, and groaned as his tongue pushed down on mine, trapping it on the floor of my mouth.

He pushed his cock through my palms, stabbing my clit with his tip.

I broke the kiss.

He looked at me with disbelief.

"I fucking need you right now, Grady." I quickly masturbated him for several seconds, then let go of him and turned around.

He breathed deeply.

I felt my ass sizzle under his stare, certain the moment was nigh.

Grady stepped right up against me, resting his erection over my ass. He grabbed my buttocks in a bunch and pushed them together over his girth. He started to grind against me.

"Yes," I moaned, suppressing an excited squeal.

"You like that, angel?"

"I love it."

He removed his shirt behind me, then stepped out of his work boots and jeans. He immediately repositioned his member between my cheeks, ground against me and spread his precum on my lower back. "You really think you can handle this?"

I hesitated.

Grady laughed, then seized hold of my sides. He spun me around. "You turn me on so much, Maxine." He smacked his lips against mine, shoving his tongue wildly inside.

I couldn't resist and rubbed my sex up to his. The size difference was astronomical. His giant balls even dwarfed my she-shaft!

His hands tore at my buttocks, plying them apart one second then forcing them together the next.

My hole was aching for attention, and each enforced closure only made my cock cravings run deeper.

Grady careered his cock against my groin.

I stumbled back a couple of steps on my stilettos, irked at the interruption to our embrace.

He pulled me back to him with one palm behind my head and the other above my ass.

I threw one thigh high and wrapped my leg around his rear.

Grady lifted me up, taking both my legs around his waist.

I hungrily kissed him.

He carried me from the kitchen into the living room.

I could feel his erection poke me between my scrotum and she-hole.

Condoms!

He devoured my tongue, sucking it into his mouth.

I had my hands hanging only gently onto his muscular shoulders, trusting he wouldn't drop me.

Grady laid me down on the sofa, then stepped back, staring at me.

"What is it?" I asked, shaking with as much uncontrollable lust as unshakeable sense of danger. "What's the matter?"

He shook his head. "Nothing." He grabbed his dick. "I just can't believe my luck."

"Your luck?"

"You're a stunning t-girl, Maxine."

I took a moment to drink in the complement, then parted my legs wide.

"I've wanted someone like you all to myself for years."

"I'm *all* yours," I insisted, and slowly lifted my rump less than half an inch into the air. "What're you going to do me, Grady?"

He brought himself next to my face. "I'm going to make you cum, Maxine." He slid his shaft over my lipstick-coated lips. "At the same time you make me cum."

I lost myself on his length.

Grady set his thighs to either side of my head, forcing my face upwards to accommodate his every inch. He penetrated me right down to my throat.

Excitement coursed through my body when he blocked my airway.

He leaned his body down on mine.

I tried to make him raise his girth to give me a chance to breathe.

He pushed his cock deeper into my orifice.

Fear seized my senses. I tried to suck in air through my nostrils to no avail. I started to see stars. What if I passed out? What if I-

Grady sucked my little clit into his mouth.

My pulse rapidly quickened.

He licked all around my sex.

I tried to gently slap his bare ass, to make him aware of my deepening dilemma.

His cock pulsated, and he thrust it further inside me.

My sphincter tightened with all-encompassing trepidation.

Grady's fingers took between my legs, reaching down and forcing my cheeks apart.

I hit him harder.

He finally relented, raising his crotch in the air.

"I couldn't breathe!" I gasped-

He shoved himself inside me again, stilling his shaft in place.

I was panicking, but my fucking clit was betraying me and suggesting absolute delight!

Grady sucked her up and down.

I wanted desperately to enjoy myself, and tried to turn my face in one direction.

He set his thigh closer.

I turned the opposite direction.

He stilled me with his other thigh.

I was trapped!

Grady lifted his length out of my mouth.

I dragged air into my lungs.

He planted his balls on my mouth.

I licked between them, eager to please as I was able to draw more oxygen in.

He flicked one fingertip over my asshole, just tapping my rosebud.

I took one of his testicles between my lips, rolling it around for several seconds, as I felt his muscular body so obviously enjoy the attention. I switched to the second ball, and his lower half vibrated against me.

Grady gave my clit the most incredible oral.

Was this my reward? Was he really going to get me off this way? I hoped so, and eagerly pumped at his mouth.

He used his fingertips to make teasing, circular motions around my hole.

I tried to manoeuvre myself to force his fingers inside me.

He lifted his balls, then slapped his length down on my face.

I took him into my mouth, finally getting to suck him hard and fast – the way I wanted!

He grunted into my sex.

I inhaled at every opportunity, fearful of total oral annihilation.

Grady seemed to understand, and began pulling his cock to the edge of my lips then gifting it back to me.

I sucked him deep down to my throat, trusting he'd withdraw far enough to allow me to draw breath.

He did, simultaneously massaging my she-member with his mouth. He teased my hole more and more, not once penetrating her despite my movements.

I worked him faster, knowing he'd cum twice already. I'd be so embarrassed to cum first. It wasn't very ladylike, and I knew Grady liked me submissive and certainly not selfish. I tried not to fuck his mouth, even though my instincts were telling me to. I could just all too easily give in, and pummel his precious lips.

Grady stabbed my throat, pinning me.

I frantically tried to free myself, clawing at his sides.

He sucked at my slit.

I made an impossible, muffled attempt at speech.

Grady ejaculated into my throat.

Where the hell were the signs? The warning!?!

I could feel his balls atop my nose, emptying.

He relented nothing of his oral onslaught on my she-shaft, sucking wildly.

I gulped down his semen.

He pulled out, spilling more on my face.

"Yes, Grady!" I cried.

He suffocated my sex with his face.

I gyrated back up into him.

His cock slipped into my mouth.

I wanted to cum before his alpha male guilt overcame him. I deserved this orgasm. I *needed* my release!

Grady relaxed the lower half of his body, concentrating all his tension on my she-rod.

I started to lick his deflating cock clean.

He was like a man possessed, flinging his face up and down on my sex.

It was incredible as I felt the deplosion first within my sphincter. I gasped on his girth. Then my she-testes tensed. I groaned. My love juice spurted up into his mandible cavern.

Grady retreated, switching from his mouth to his palm, and masturbated me through my climax.

"Oh my God, Grady!" I squealed.

He dribbled my cum back down on my crotch.

I spilled more from my slit between his fingers. "You drive me so crazy!"

He laughed, then held my little clit up so he could lick her clean.

"Thank you, thank you, thank you."

He kissed my sex. "It was my pleasure, angel." His cock throbbed against the side of my face. "But I promise you that'll be your last orgasm with direct stimulation."

I tried to look down at him, breathless.

"Make no mistake about it, Maxine, I *will* fuck the cum out of you next time."

CHAPTER 27

I awoke to warmth. It was Grady's naked body next to mine. He was on his back. I was on my side, naked from my chest down with my red swimsuit riding high, one arm and one leg draped across him.

Daylight shone in on the bedroom.

I threw my eyes to the window.

No one was there. Not that person. Not that Dominic.

There was still some wind and the clouds suggested it wouldn't be long until there was more rain. But the storm had passed.

Grady groaned in his sleep.

I wondered if he was dreaming, then reached for his rod, wrapping my fingers around the girth. I just adored the feel of him in my palm. He was so big. And so fat. It was a pleasure just to hold. Except only holding it wouldn't do. I wanted to move it. So I did.

His face twitched.

I squeezed his cock, then released it temporarily to move the duvet off his body. I gazed at his physique with lust. He was so ruggedly handsome. And, even though his country ways made him so different to the men I'd been with before, I fancied him like crazy.

He smiled as I took him in my hand again.

"Are you awake?" I whispered.

Grady ignored me.

"Okay." I set his cock up high. "Sweet dreams." I began to jerk his erection.

I slurped on my lover's tongue as my hand flew up and down on his member. I could feel his convulsions pulsate from his penis to his lips when he broke the kiss.

"Oh, angel!" he cried.

I grinned. "You gonna cum for me?"

He nodded profusely, fucking my fist.

I kept my hand firm on his cock, as I pulled my red swimsuit over my head then rolled onto my front. "You take over, Grady."

"What?"

"I can't make you cum where I want you to... From this angle."

He panted. "Where do you want me to cum, Maxine?"

I let go of him.

He grabbed his manhood, and furiously masturbated himself as he gazed at my nude body.

"On my ass," I insisted, half-turning it towards him.

His face flushed red.

"Come on, sir. Give me that warm, hot cum. I want it all over these cheeks of mine." I slid my fingers to my buttocks, then pulled my cheeks apart.

Grady gazed at my hole.

"So what if some gets on my ass pussy?"

He vigorously pumped himself.

"Do it, Grady. Spunk on my pussy. I need to feel it. I *want* to feel it!"

"I wish I had the condoms in here, baby."

I giggled. "I've already told you it's okay to cum across my ass."

"No, Maxine." Sweat trickled down his face. "I don't want to just cum on your ass." His chest was bright red with the force of his fist. "I want to cum *in* it." He pummelled his huge member. "I want to *fuck* your ass pussy until I..." Grady shot his hot sperm over my rear.

I pulled my cheeks further apart.

"Oh fuck!" he yelled, cumming across my flesh.

I aimed my hole at his shaft, striving to collect more.

"Jesus, baby!"

"More!" I shouted, almost irate as his lashings landed everywhere but directly on my target.

Grady pounded his massive penis.

I dug my fingernails into my skin. "Cum on my pussy!"

He shot a volley high onto my lower back, then wheezed himself to a standstill.

I was as flattered as I was frustrated. Perhaps more so the latter. But still I smiled, satisfied I turned him on so much.

Grady took a forceful yet careful hold of my hair, then gently pulled my mouth towards his, kissing my soft lips.

I happily returned his affection, as I lifted my torso to give him my all. I was delighted when I felt his sperm slide down from my lower back to between my butt crack.

He held me back by my hair, as he parted our lips and breathed deeply in and out. "You're incredible, Maxine. What a wake-up call."

I ran my fingertips over his tummy. "My pleasure, Grady."

The silence of the room only seemed to emphasise the elephant in it.

"The storm's over," I whispered.

"Yes." He caressed my face. "You're so beautiful."

"Thank you." I ran my fingers through his navel hair. "Grady, can we drive out to find my sister Jenny's car today?"

"The pink fuck mobile?"

I rolled my eyes. "I really want to see what it's like."

"I understand."

"I'm deeply worried about it."

"Angel, stop worrying. I'll take you out to see it this morning. Okay?"

I nodded. "You didn't see it yesterday?"

"Yesterday?"

I felt his sperm sticking between my buttocks, just above my hole. "When you... Stormed off... When I told you about..."

"Nick," Grady said, then scratched himself between his shaft and his scrotum.

"Did you see the car?"

Grady shook his head. "I didn't go that way."

I nibbled my lower lip. "Did you see him?"

He said nothing.

"Did you see Nick?"

Grady leaned one leg out of the bed.

I put my hand on his arm. "Whatever you tell me, it won't change a thing between us. I'm here. You have me."

He watched my eyes for an age.

Was he checking me for sincerity? For conscientiousness? Or was it for-

"I drove past his house, Max."

I cringed.

"Max*ine*, sorry."

I twirled his hair in my forefinger. "Did you see him?"

Grady succumbed to a nod.

Tension took hold of my insides.

"But I didn't go in," he said. "I didn't see the point. Like you said, I have you."

I ignored a foreboding sense of being his prisoner.

"I didn't speak to him, baby. Yes, I was jealous, but I realised I was being stupid. Besides, I knew Nick's dad very well when we were growing up. It wouldn't have been right to start shit with him over you."

I agreed, although something in his tone made me sound less than worthy. I ignored it.

"I do have something to tell you, though." Grady threw both his legs to the floor, stretched, then stood. "I went to see Dominic instead."

My stomach churned.

He confidently turned his naked body towards me. "Don't look at me like that, angel."

"Like what?" I snapped, as his semen seeped deeper into my crevice.

"Like you're pissed off with me."

"Did you tell him about me?"

Grady nodded.

I looked to the bedroom window again. "You'd no need to do that."

"I had to tell someone, angel." He rested his hands on his hips. "Don't you understand? I'm happy. I'm over the moon!"

I crawled to the other edge of the bed, and lowered my feet to the floor, careful not to stain the sheets with his cum. "Well, I absolutely do *not* want to meet him under any circumstances, Grady. I don't like the sound of him at all." I found wipes, and began to clean my rear as he watched me. "And if you've any thoughts of sharing me in a threesome with your friend, you can positively forget them. Whatever favours you think you owe him for bringing you shemales from the city, you won't be using me to repay him."

Grady sighed.

I put the wipes in the bin.

"You know what day it is, Maxine?"

I looked at his fat girth. Was it fuck day? Really? Would he finally take my ass pussy?

"It's panty day, which means you get to wear some sexy underwear."

My chest inflated as I inhaled.

"Didn't you notice the two sports bags I brought home last

night?" he asked.

I had.

"Aren't you curious to find out what's in them, baby?"

CHAPTER 28

I was sat in the passenger seat of Grady's car, a spotless red BMW roadster, in a short black leather skirt with my stocking and suspender-clad legs crossed. He'd eagerly sprung the surprise of the sports bags upon me, revealing beautiful sets of lingerie he'd brought from Dominic's home, and begged me to wear something for when he took me out to investigate my sister's car. I was reluctant to go out dressed as a girl, but his kisses on my neck had weakened my resolve and here I was kitted out like a city slut. Even my stocking tops were visible at the end of my skirt.

"Angel," he said, his voice higher than normal, "can I ask you a question?"

"Yes, Grady."

"Is there anything you're particularly fond of in the bedroom that I don't know about?"

I thought for several seconds, then grinned. "I like having my ass worshipped. It makes me feel so sexy."

He adjusted his jeans. "I'll remember that."

"In gay parlance, I'd be a bottom..."

He grunted.

"... But I no longer see myself that way..."

He tapped the steering wheel.

"... I'm a girl now."

Grady smiled. "Permanently?"

I thought about it. Did he mean permanently his girl? Or just in general? "I have to find my sister's car first."

He looked ahead.

I moved in my seat, and placed my hand on his leg. "Is Grady your first name or your last name?"

"Why, baby, you think you're going to have to provide a statement to the police?"

Fear paralysed every part of me but my throbbing clit. How could he have such control over her? And over me?

"There it is," he said, gesturing ahead.

I sat back in Grady's car, with the passenger door open and my stiletto heels set on the ground as he looked over my sister's car.

He looked so ruggedly handsome as he inspected the vehicle. So manly. So sex on legs my clit was stiff, despite my worries as even I could tell there was damage to the bodywork.

"Is it bad?"

Grady ignored me.

"Sir," I called. "I need to know."

"Give me a moment," he snapped, looking momentarily between my open legs, "woman."

I knew even my balls were too big for my revealing g-string, and quickly crossed my legs. My sex rubbed the lace fabric.

Grady spent several minutes looking over my sister's car.

I looked around the area, my mind replaying the moment I'd almost lost my life here.

My hero had saved me.

I wondered if he could save my skin when it came to the car-

"I'll not lie to you, angel, this could be a write-off." He was holding the key to the car in his hand.

"It can't be, Grady! She'll kill me!"

"It starts."

I'd heard the engine. I wasn't that stupid of a sissy.

"But I'm reluctant to move it. You'd be best calling for roadside assistance."

I checked up and down the road. It was clear. I stood out of the car.

Grady grinned.

"You know I've no charge in my mobile. And you've no phone."

He took hold of my hand, pulling me to him. "Dominic has a phone in his house. I could take you there."

My eyes bloated. "No, you will *not*. I'm not going to his-"

Grady slipped his tongue into my mouth.

I melted like a wanton whore, instinctively ignoring the outdoor surroundings.

He kissed me gently.

I tried to drag passion out from him.

His nostrils flared. His hands slid to my skirt.

I tried to stop him.

Grady seized both my arms with one palm.

I opened my eyes.

He opened his.

I tried to shake my head.

He dragged me into a deeper, luscious kiss.

I surrendered.

My lover snaked my skirt to my hips in broad daylight.

I closed my eyes.

Grady gently caressed my rear, lovingly tending to buttocks freshly washed from his morning supply of semen.

I groaned.

He slid his thumb into the string of my underwear, retrieving it from between my cheeks.

I listened to the sounds of nature around us.

Grady sensually parted his lips from mine.

I involuntarily released a whining sound. I was needy. I knew it. And I could feel my skin reddening because of it.

"I'm going to worship this fine, fine ass of yours," he said, pushing his palm more forcefully on my rear.

I stumbled forward, as he stepped aside.

He pushed me over towards the front of the car, at the same time releasing my arms.

My palms fell flat on the pink bodywork.

The sunlight reflected off the glass.

He moved behind me.

"Here, Grady?"

"Yes."

I wheezed. "Aren't you embarrassed someone will see?"

"No, slut."

"But aren't you embarrassed to be seen with someone like me?" I demanded, looking over my shoulder at him.

"*Like* you? Maybe." He smiled. "But never *you*. Not ever, angel." He crouched behind me, and eased my legs apart.

"Someone could come along!"

"Someone, angel?" He pulled my g-string down my thighs to below my stocking tops.

"Anyone!"

Grady took hold of my testicles in one hand. "You said someone." He breathed over my hole. "Did you have someone in particular in my mind?"

"What? No!"

He fondled my genitalia. "Were you thinking of Nick?"

"Are you crazy, Grady-"

He licked between my ass cheeks.

"Oh God... No... I don't even know what he looks like..."

He tested my rosebud with the tip of his tongue.

"I don't care what he looks like."

Grady laughed. "You were still going to fuck him."

I couldn't dignify that truth with an answer.

He extended his forefinger from my balls to my erect clit, pushing her up.

I tried not to touch the car with my fingernails, fearful of damaging it further.

Grady expertly drove his tongue into my entrance.

"Yes, Grady, just like that." I looked up the road, then down.

He swirled around the inner edges of my opening.

"You eat my she-pussy so good."

He gave a manly, know-it-all chuckle, then prodded deeper, juggling my testes at the same time.

"May I milk my sex?"

He nodded between my buns.

I didn't hesitate, seizing my she-shaft in my wanking hand.

Grady pinned her up and back against the flesh of my lower abdomen.

I hadn't the strength in my whole hand to overpower his single digit.

He lapped at my sphincter in swift, circular motions.

I wrapped my second hand around my clit.

He released her, then took playfully patted at my little love-balls.

I was squirming my ass against his face. "I can't believe I'm letting you do this to me out here," I said quietly. "Anyone could catch us." I stroked my sex. "*Someone* could."

He rounded the shape of his tongue, then hastily attempted to feed it back and forth through my anal tunnel.

I gasped, adoring every sensation within. "Yes, Grady, I mean what I'm saying... *Someone* could catch us."

He remained silent but for the audible motions of his tongue-fucking.

"I wouldn't even know Nick if he was watching us."

Grady brought the fingers of his free hand between my thighs, teasing the sensitivity of my soft skin.

I masturbated myself with more vigour, glancing at the trees all around us. "Dominic could be watching us."

He removed his tongue. "You wouldn't know him."

I thought of the person at the window. "I think I would-"

Grady fired two of his fingers violently into my anus.

I screeched.

He stilled me in place by my balls.

I pumped my she-penis, bending my knees slightly for better balance.

My lover rigged up a rancid concoction of pain and pleasure within the walls of my rectum.

"I don't care if they see us," I lied. "I think I even want them to."

He snarled beneath me.

"Yeah, it's true."

Grady planted his mouth on one cheek, striving to suck a love bite onto the surface of my skin.

"Part of me gets off on being out here."

He turned his fingers inside me.

"On perhaps being seen."

He twisted, then added a third.

"Or caught."

There was the distant sound of a passenger aeroplane in the sky above.

Grady tried to push a fourth finger inside.

"Only your cock can stretch me that much-"

He succeeded.

I splurged precum onto my sister's car.

"Is this enough worship for you?" he growled.

I couldn't answer.

He licked at my ass cheek.

I tried to look around, as dizziness almost threatened my balance.

Grady careered his four fingers in and out of me.

My g-string at my thighs stopped me from spreading my legs further.

A cow made a sound in an unseen field somewhere behind some trees.

I no longer cared about anything other than my impending

orgasm.

Grady let go of my little balls.

I relished the freedom, took a firmer hold of my clitty in one hand and steadied myself on the car with the other.

"This pink fuck mobile," he said, spilling saliva on my ass, "brought you to me, angel. We're meant to be."

I giggled, my anus widening for more of his onslaught.

"You're supposed to be mine, Maxine."

I was ploughing my foreskin back and forth.

"I want you always to be mine!"

The beautiful weather lit up my joy as I took aim at the bonnet of my sister Jenny's car.

"I want you to stay with me!"

Pleasure was overriding all sense of agony in my ass.

"I want you to *want* to stay with me!"

My stiffness was about to summon she-spunk from within my tensing scrotum.

"Say it, Maxine!"

"I... I... I..."

"Say it!" He slammed his hand into my rear.

Perspiration slid down my skin.

"Now!"

"I'm yours," I squealed, knowing my words were not enough for him and embracing my own convoluted desires and demands. "But this..." I heaved. "This isn't worship." I panted. "This is debauchery!"

His hand half fell from within my sphincter.

I looked at my little length protruding from my grip.

"Max-"

"Ine!"

He formed his fingers into a fist, then tried to drive them back up into me.

I clenched. I gasped. I set my eyes on my sex. "Oh, Grady!" I watched as my she-sperm volleyed out onto the car, showering it in copious amounts unbefitting of one challenged to champion femininity.

Grady twisted his fingers free from fist-form, then hooked hold of my hole.

My prostate reacted, erupting yet more love juice onto the pink bodywork.

His breathing was ragged.

My thoughts were despicable.

Grady tried to work more out from within me.

I let go of my clit.

He slowed inside me.

I had both palms on the car.

He came to a stop.

I was still too.

"I want you to stay with me," he whispered.

I couldn't.

"But I won't lie to you..."

He what?

"The car's fine."

He carefully removed his fingers.

"There's superficial damage. Scrapes to the rear. A brake light's out. But nothing that can't be tended to in a few minutes."

I exhaled deeply. Minutes?

"It's driveable." He pulled my skirt down at my rear. "You can go."

Go? Go where? Home? Now? After this? After that? After all the this and that?

"I won't stop you, angel."

CHAPTER 29

I drove slowly behind Grady's BMW roadster, paranoid any kind of unseen damage to the chassis of my sister's car had made it dangerous to drive.

He'd been pretty sure everything was right with it, even tiring of my constant questions to the point where he took himself to his own car and left me standing at hers.

I'd jumped quickly in, then followed him.

Driving a manual car in stilettos was different, admittedly.

My ass was so sensitive to every country bump in the road and still my little clit was leaking wetness into the lace of my g-string.

I knew it was time to go home. Even without a charge in my mobile, I'd find the main road sooner or later. It was daytime. The storm was long over.

All I'd to go to his cottage for was to change out of these super sexy clothes and back into the dirty, dreaded male ones I'd arrived in.

Grady indicated to turn left.

I did the same, recognising the lane from earlier.

We were nearly there.

My sister still wouldn't be home for another couple of days-

No, slut, you have to get her car to a garage and pay to get it fixed!

Maybe I could stay just one more night with my Grady.

You've no idea how much permanent damage there could actually be!

Perhaps even just a few hours this afternoon?

It could be a write-off after all!

I swerved to avoid a pothole. My sister's car responded as it should. I straightened the steering wheel.

You're not a fucking mechanic, you cock-hungry whore!

I watched Grady make a right towards the grounds of his cottage, then speeding a little ahead of me.

I missed him immediately.

How could I be feeling like this already?

I quickly sped up to catch him.

How could I feel a temporary ache in my heart when he almost sped out of view?

I chased up behind him.

Grady's brake lights came on.

I eased my foot on my own brake.

He parked up.

I drew alongside him.

He threw open his door.

I watched his strong chest. I wanted him so much. This was insane! No man had ever had such an effect on me. And certainly not so soon. Where was my head at to be letting a silly little thing like feelings come over me?

He gave me a wink.

I wanted to give him a wank.

"See you inside?" he called.

I shook my head.

There was instantaneous horror on his face. Poor guy.

I opened my door, set my heels on the ground and stepped out. "Don't you dare go in without walking me inside with you, Grady," I said.

He walked around my sister's car, then linked his arm with mine. "May I, young lady?" he asked.

I couldn't help myself. I leaned my lips to his. I felt fireworks inside as we kissed.

He parted his lips first.

I felt such need when I looked at him again.

His face gave something away, I just wasn't sure what.

"Say something," I begged, hoping he'd tell me he was finally going to fuck me. I just needed to pamper myself. To shower a little of the pain away from my asshole.

"Are you going to get your things and leave now?" he asked.

I hesitated.

"It's been fun, angel. It has. And you're welcome to stay. I *want* you to stay. But-"

"You haven't fucked me."

Birds tweeted. A gentle breeze blew over us.

I tapped one stiletto heel off a stone.

"No," he said.

"Why not, Grady?"

"Not yet."

"I want you to. I don't want to leave here without feeling your cock throb inside me."

He smiled. "And I don't want you to leave until I've made you cum through that stimulation alone."

Impossible.

"But..."

Why was there always a but?

"You stayed the night again." He was reaching for his cigarettes. "So you've built up plenty of chores to take care of."

I groaned.

"Nothing's free in this life, Maxine."

I sighed.

"Understand me?"

I nodded. "What would you like me to do for you... Sir?"

CHAPTER 30

Perspiration enveloped my scantily-clad body as I continued to mow the last lawn of one of Grady's vast gardens.

I couldn't believe how hard he'd worked me. I could feel muscles I never knew I had absolutely ache. This was not labour befitting of a sissy!

Occasional clouds were my only respite from a strong sun in stark contrast to the storm which had trapped me here.

My sister's car was parked around the other side of the cottage. I was trapped only by my kinky desires to finally have him inside me.

My anus was so sore from that morning's finger-fucking over the car.

I sneezed. Surely it was too early in the year for hay fever? Well, it was in the city. But what about in the country? I'd heard before about different concentrations of pollen. Different types too. Was cutting all this grass the stupidest thing I could do for my allergy?

I pushed on, knowing I was so nearly finished.

I wanted nothing more than to just stagger inside, slip off my bright neon blue, string bikini and spend a good twenty to thirty minutes in the shower. My body needed to heal.

The sun was beginning to set.

Could I really fit in that long coveted fuck I so desperately wanted before I set off on my way?

Would my ass even be fit to take it?

I finally finished, slumping over the lawnmower and taking a well-earned breather.

There was a wolf-whistle from the nearby lane.

I looked over my arms to see Grady strolling back from his mother's cottage. I surrendered to an exhausted smile.

He approached, looking as handsome and rugged as ever, casting his eyes over the garden. "You finished at last?" he asked.

I stared daggers at him.

"I'll not be harsh, baby." He was still surveying my work. "It's not a great job. Your first time?"

"No," I lied.

"You were terribly slow."

I adjusted my clit in my skimpy bikini bottoms.

Grady watched, then fondled his mammoth sex through his jeans, emphasising the gargantuan outline.

"Are you hard *again*?" I asked.

"Semi, sweetheart."

I smiled.

"You turn me on so much."

I almost told him not to get used to it, then thought much, much better of it. "Let me see it."

"Why, Maxine?"

"Because I want to see it. I need to see it. I haven't seen it since this morning." I swapped my balance from one white sandal-clad foot to the other.

He put his hand on his fly.

"I think I've earned it."

His hand stilled.

"Show me it."

He said nothing.

"Please, Grady." I gestured to the lawn. "Look what I did."

He shrugged.

"I did *all* your gardens."

He pursed his lips, then nodded. "Okay, but only because you're so hot." He unzipped his fly.

"Unbutton your jeans," I pleaded. "I want to see it in all it's glory."

Grady, to my surprise, obeyed me. Then he pulled down the front of his boxers, allowing his huge cock to burst into view.

My jaw dropped without me even realising, at first. "Magnificent," I whispered, gazing at its amazing girth and sheer phenomenal length. "It's just so big, sir."

He grinned.

I slid my fingers into the rear of my bikini bottoms, gently caressing my cheeks, then pulled the material out from my crack where it'd tightened during my toiling.

Grady just let his cock sit out in the sunset.

"I want it."

It was stiffening.

"I'm so thirsty." I'd run out of water. "But it's my ass that's crying out for that thing, Grady."

He nodded.

My little clitty was growing too.

"You're a bad girl, Maxine."

"Why don't we take ourselves inside?" I suggested. "I'll take a quick shower, then we can get ourselves more comfortable." I was sore, but I needed to know how he felt inside me before I went home.

"You'll do no such thing."

No shower? "You want me all sweaty and dirty?" Why did that turn me on so much? "Okay, Grady, anything you want." I started to reach for his member.

"No touching, angel."

I swallowed saliva. "Okay, sir."

"Put the lawnmower away, then follow me inside. You've a whole list of chores to get on with inside."

"What?" I asked.

"When you finish them, *then* you can have your shower."

What the hell was he talking about? I was exhausted. I didn't have the energy for more chores. I'd done enough.

Grady took hold of his shaft. "If you're still standing after all that, *then* you can have this."

I'd pass out if I exerted myself anymore.

He leaned forward, pecking my lips. "And, if you can't stand, you can just lie down... On your front."

Go home, sissy. Get out of here. He's a psycho.

"And I'll fuck that she-pussy of yours 'til you cum, baby."

CHAPTER 31

My bikini bottoms were riding right up at the crack of my ass while simultaneously cutting into my scrotum. I couldn't be bothered fixing it for what would've felt like the thousandth time. My clit was lifeless. Deflated. Numb.

And every additional menial chore had me begging for my bed.

"You're almost finished, angel," Grady said gently, staring at my ass. "I made sure to leave you warm water for your shower." He was stood in just a towel, his body still wet from his own shower and his hair still matted to his skin.

My clitty didn't have the energy to react, but my mind and my heart did. "I can barely stand, Grady... Please help me."

He came over to me, then took the brush from me. "You only had to ask."

"What?"

"I'd have helped you all day."

I was in disbelief.

"It's a man's honour to help his woman, Maxine. Us country boys know you city folk are different. I didn't want to offend you by offering." He began to sweep the kitchen floor.

I had to use the edge of the table to keep myself from collapsing.

He took a matter of seconds to finish sweeping, then scooped up the crumbs into the bin. "Finished," he said, then had the audacity to pass me the brush.

I took it without thinking.

"You're free to take your shower."

"Thanks, sir." I cursed myself for my subordination, then turned, my every muscle and bone aching. I trudged across the floor, leaving the brush by the door, and headed up the hall.

"Maxine," he called.

I was in pain as I turned to look at him watching me.

"Untie your bikini before you go into the bathroom."

I didn't have the strength to argue, and slowly reached up to remove my top, letting it fall to the floor.

"And those," he said, pointing at my bottoms.

I turned from him, embarrassed at how small and soft my clit felt. I didn't want him to see her. "Okay." I carefully untied the bottoms, freeing them from my crotch and allowing them too to slip away.

"You *are* beautiful, baby."

"Thank you. I'm so tired, Grady. You worked me hard today."

"The night's still young."

I bent over to pick up my bikini.

He wheezed.

I could feel my anus stretch as I stooped. "It's not young, Grady. Not for me. I'm ready for bed."

He giggled. "You're so horny, Maxine."

No, I wasn't. I was genuinely exhausted. I would be going to bed to sleep.

"Enjoy your shower. Then change into the clothes I've left out for you in the bedroom and meet me back in the living room. We can have a cuddle before bedtime."

I walked into the bathroom, lacking even the energy to close the door behind me.

"You're a really good girl, Maxine."

I felt manipulated. And totally at his mercy. I was unable – and somewhat unwilling – to leave tonight.

And not only because it was so late and I was so tired.

Some deep part of me was really beginning to believe I was exactly where I was supposed to be. And that I was supposed to stay.

And in spite of myself.

CHAPTER 32

I lathered my body in soap, repeatedly, as the hot water rushed down my slender back and bottom. The sensations were heavenly, easing my aches.

The bathroom window creaked. I put it down the to age of the cottage rather than the weather, which was still calm.

I turned my front to the shower head, letting the stream wash away the soap down my skin.

Grady whistled somewhere out of sight.

I was still so tired. If he'd had a bath in his home instead of a shower I could've fallen asleep in it.

I reminded myself I'd already nearly died from drowning once in the last few days.

I rubbed more soap into my fingers, then massaged it into my opposing arms.

My clit bobbed gently as I moved.

I'd enjoyed my orgasm in the morning. Thoroughly. I was more surprised by my ease at behaving so in public – albeit a quiet, country public – than I was shocked by the fact it'd happened. Or, rather, I'd let it happen.

Oh, angel, how I'm going to love you. You're a born subordinate.

The bathroom door was closed.

He was sweet, giving me my privacy. Although he could've taken my bikini out to the laundry basket for me, if he really wanted to get in my good books.

Who was I kidding?

You're supposed to be mine, Maxine.

Grady didn't seek my approval.

I want you always to be mine!

He was the man of the house.

I want you to stay with me!

I was the lady.

I want you to want *to stay with me!*

The sissy.

Say it, Maxine!

The sleepover slut.

You can go.

The one who'd be leaving first thing in the morning.

I won't stop you, angel.

Perhaps before he even awoke.

I heard classical music playing as I left the bathroom for the bedroom. I made nothing of it, and walked on in to get changed for him. I was still very tired, but my shower had slightly reinvigorated me. Besides, one last cuddle on the sofa with Grady was actually very, very appealing.

I saw what he'd left out for me to wear. My heart warmed. Such good taste.

The window caught my attention for a moment too long.

It was too dark outside to know if someone was out there watching me. The lights in the bedroom only lit up inside. If someone was out there, they could see all of me. *All* of me. I was completely naked.

I ran my hands down my body. Yes, I'd show them, this was *my* body. Mine. I was claiming it rightfully.

The classical music hit a loud crescendo down the hall. It was *very* loud.

I quickly lifted the sexy red negligee from the bed and stepped into it. It was a bodysuit, requiring me to put it on in such a manner. The lace fitted snugly around my clit and girly balls.

I moaned my approval.

It felt so classy, like there was a chance Grady really did respect me.

You only had to ask.

Oh God, what if I still heard his voice in my head even after I'd left him?

I'd have helped you all day.

I stepped into a ridiculously high-heeled pair of red stilettos. They propped me up at least five inches higher than my natural height. But I felt so sexy in them. I touched, then groped my own ass. The shoes really did make it stick right out. I was certain Grady would love it!

I'd my make-up practically perfected within twenty minutes, only my tiredness slowing me down.

I looked at the bed, longing to get in and just drift off-

Meet me back in the living room.

I did want that cuddle. One last cuddle before this crazy experience drew to a natural close. Besides, I'd probably fall asleep in his loving arms in front of the TV.

I gave myself a final once over in the mirror, then headed out to the hall.

Despite the volume of the music, I could've sworn I heard Grady laugh loudly. I wondered what he was watching.

I walked confidently into the living room with my hands propped on my hips and looked at him sat up on the sofa, smiling at me. "Well?" I asked. "Does sir approve?"

He nodded. "Gentlemen?"

I didn't understand the comment, as I began to turn around in front of him, eager to hear his reaction when he saw the emphasised shape of my ass on my stil-

Two men were stood in the kitchen staring right at me.

I froze.

The music was suddenly lowered.

"Grady, who the fuck are they?" I demanded, stepping backwards towards the sofa.

Grady stood up.

I bumped right into him behind me.

He put his hands on my bare arms.

He's a psycho.

I knew that face.

They're going to rape you.

I'd seen it before.

Then kill you.

"Gentlemen," Grady began, "this is Maxine."

Then burn Jenny's car.

"Hello, Maxine," they said in unison.

I couldn't take my eyes off them. Fear multiplied as I looked between them. One young. One older. Even older than Grady, I guessed.

"She's the girl who's turned my world upside down," he added.

Girl? I could feel their eyes between my legs. On my small, shrivelled clit hidden with the lace confines of the bodysuit. I had my legs tight together.

Grady rubbed my arms with his thumbs. "Maxine, I'd like to

introduce you to Dominic." He began to gesture to the older of the two.

I couldn't say anything.

Dominic smiled at me.

"And this is his son..."

His son smiled too. "Hey, Maxine," he said.

"... Nick."

He was Nick!?! Oh my God! My Nick! The Nick I'd spoken to online. The Nick I was supposed to be meeting up with just a few nights ago for a quick one-on-one sex session. "I know you," I said, and felt Grady's grip tighten. "I've seen you before. At the window. You were looking in at me."

A tense silence reverberated throughout the room.

"Now, now, Maxine," Grady said, "be nice. Nick's been good enough to bring over a charger for your phone."

It was sat on the kitchen table.

"I should apologise," Nick said.

"Yes, son, you should," added Dominic, tutting.

"That was me at the window. I shouldn't have been looking. I'm very, very sorry. To both of you. Sorry, Maxine. Sorry, Grady."

Grady slipped his arms around my tight waist. "It's forgotten about, Nick, isn't it, Maxine?"

I could barely find my voice. "Yes." It sure as hell was not!

"Go wait in the car," Dominic told his son. "I'll be out shortly."

Shortly?

"Yes, dad," Nick said, and hurried out the front door, slamming it behind him.

Shortly frightened me. Shortly allowed enough time to do all manner of sordid things to my vulnerable body.

"What can I say, Grady?" Dominic began taking steps from the kitchen into the living room. "You've netted yourself a very beautiful, young lady here." His eyes again took to my crotch. "So much more natural than some of the ones I've brought here before."

I could feel Grady's groin right up against my rump.

"I only wish I could tell you she was here to stay," Grady said.

Dominic came to within two footsteps in front of me. "I'm sure she will. You make quite the couple."

My heart was pounding.

"Don't be afraid, Maxine. We're not monsters out here in the country. Am I making you uncomfortable?”

Yes. “No.”

“You're not going to up and leave my friend Grady here, are you?”

I couldn't answer.

“That's your car outside? What was it you called it, Grady, the pink-”

“Never mind that now, Dominic,” Grady interrupted. “Tell Nick thank you for the charger.”

Dominic licked his lips right in front of me. Then he gave a fake laugh. “I get the hint, Grady. I don't blame you.” His eyes were all over my torso. “I wouldn't want to share her either.”

“I'm right here,” I said, unsure of where I'd found such defiance.

Dominic stepped back. “My apologies, Maxine.” He shook his head. “I'm too used to paying for it, I forget there's a real person underneath.”

I ever so slightly moved my buttocks against my man's groin. “Grady would *never* have to pay for it with me. I'm his lady.” I half-turned to look at him. “And he's my man.”

Dominic tipped his hat. “I bid you both adieu.”

“Goodnight, mate,” Grady said.

I could feel him grow against me.

Dominic saw himself out.

Grady and I stood in silence.

His erection poked harder against me.

I said nothing. I knew he wanted to fuck me. I kind of wanted him to fuck me. But I was so tired. And anxious from just meeting those two like that.

Their car started outside.

“I'm falling for you,” he said.

They drove away.

I rubbed his forearms.

“It's okay,” he said. “You don't need to say it back... I know I'm cruel with the chores.”

I loosened his grip just enough so I could turn around within his arms and look at him. “Yes, you are. I don't mind pulling my weight. I really don't. I'd cook and clean for you all day long. But that physical labour is too much. It really is, Grady. I'm exhausted.” I felt his cock through his jeans. “This should be going up inside me tonight."

"It will. I'm going to keep my promise to you, angel. I will make you cum from penetration alone."

I shook my head. "Let's go to bed."

He let me lead him by the hand to the bedroom.

"I'm shattered," I whispered, then collapsed onto the bed.

Grady started to unbutton his flannel shirt.

I was face down on the duvet. I hadn't the energy to even watch him, never mind climb under the duvet.

"I want you so much, Maxine."

My eyes were shut. I was drifting off. "Grady, I'm leaving tomorrow."

He sighed.

"In the morning..."

He threw his shirt in the corner.

"... First thing."

He unbuckled his jeans.

But I was asleep before they even hit the floor.

CHAPTER 33

My mouth was dry. But my head was clear. My eyes were on Grady sleeping next to me in his boxer shorts.

I checked him. He wasn't erect.

There was only a hint of oncoming daylight coming through the window. It was perhaps even early for a country farm boy.

I was still on top of the duvet, still wearing my negligee bodysuit and five inch stiletto heels, but I knew what I had to do. Jenny would be home all too soon, tomorrow to be precise. I couldn't trust myself to really leave if he was awake.

I carefully slid off my side of the bed.

My side. That hurt to think of it that way, given I was leaving it behind.

I silently crept around the bed, then sneaked past Grady towards the hall.

He was snoring, as if in a genuine deep sleep.

It pained me to ignore him this way, but I slipped out of my stilettos to curb the noise and walked on regardless. I was arrogant enough to let my thoughts go with the *he'll thank me someday for this* line.

I entered the kitchen-cum-living room in search of the male clothes I'd arrived in. I checked behind the laundry basket. They weren't there, but I knew I'd left them here somewhere. Somewhere where they'd be easily retrieved, although somewhere not in plain sight so both Grady and I could temporarily forget my truth.

I spun on my bare heel and put my hands on my lace-enclosed hips. Where the fuck were they?

Nick's charger was still sat on the kitchen table.

And, strangely, my mobile phone was right beside it.

I hadn't placed it there. Had Grady? When? Had he got up during the night? Or was it already there when Nick and Dominic called to the door?

I lifted both and found a spare socket by the kettle. I flicked the switch, then watched life breath back into my phone. I looked at the kettle. I really could do with a coffee before I got on my way.

No! The sound of the kettle could wake Grady. He could walk in here in just his boxers, showing off those muscles as he moved, and tell me today's the day he was finally going to fuck me.

My mobile lit up with several messages going back days.

Mostly meaningless chat from friends. My bank were changing the rate on my overdraft. Jenny had said she'd need her car back the day she got home. She'd texted twice again asking me had I got the first text. Hell, there was even some messages going back to the night of the storm from Nick! His last one called me a cock teasing slut!

I wondered did he have any idea the *gurl* he met last night was the same Max he'd been hoping to bury his cock in that fateful night.

I didn't reply.

I needed to find my clothes.

Another text arrived. Newly sent. Not a catch-up message. It was from Jenny, confirming her flight was in the early AM tomorrow.

I needed to get out of here before I'd a change of heart, and even the sensual manner in which the rear of my negligee was massaging my hole, emphasising how quickly it'd recovered from yesterday's fisting, was only adding to my temptation to stay. To wake him. To rouse and *a*rouse him from his slumber. To find out what it was like to get a fuck from such an experienced alpha male.

I looked more frantically for my clothes, checking the living room too, before I gave up and surmised they must be in the bathroom or the bedroom.

I was even prepared to give up, grab one of Grady's long coats and just drive the so-called pink fuck mobile home without them. I really didn't care that much if people saw me like this. I had more male clothes to change into at home, and there'd be the added bonus of having this outfit to keep.

And to wear it for no one...

My clothes weren't in the bathroom.

No one at all.

I took a deep breath, ignoring my discarded stilettos in the hall, before I dared walk back into the bedroom.

Grady was still in bed, lying on his side, facing the door. His eyes were open on me.

"Hi," I whispered.

"Hi."

The mood was so different.

He coughed into his hand.

"I put my phone on charge." I pointed towards the kitchen for no real reason, and somehow it just made me feel I was doing something I shouldn't. Something which made me feel guilty.

"I heard you get up."

"You were snoring, Grady."

"I heard you."

I swallowed.

"I heard you all 'round the house. You're looking for your clothes... The one's you came in, right?"

I nodded.

"They're in here," he said.

I saw them. "Did you hide-" I cut myself off, suddenly remembering they were exactly where *I'd* left them.

"You're leaving?"

Why was he making this so hard? "I have to, Grady." Why wouldn't he just call me angel? "My sister's back first thing tomorrow morning." Then beckon me back to his bed? "I need to get her car to her."

"I see. Our little fantasy is over."

Fantasy?

He grimaced.

"Grady, if you'd heard me get as far as the front door, would you have stopped me?" I asked, nervously twiddling my thumb. "Would you have hurt me?"

He propped himself up on one elbow. "Stopped you? I don't think so. I can't promise. My heart wanted me to stop you the whole time I lay here. My head told me not to." He hesitated. "But hurt you? No, Maxine, I could never hurt you."

My body was still sore from yesterday's chores.

"Never like that, angel."

I felt my resolve weaken.

"I didn't want to hurt you last night. Quite the opposite. But you were so tired."

"I know." And whose fault was that? "I wanted it to happen, Grady. I did."

He pulled back the duvet.

I looked at his bulge, but I knew I had to go.

"Should I see you out?" he asked.

I looked at my clothes. The sight of them – male – made me almost sick to the pit of my stomach.

"You look beautiful, baby."

I smiled, just a little, knowing my make-up probably wasn't what it should be after sleeping in it.

"Should I?"

"You did promise, Grady."

"I promised?"

"Yes. You did." I fixed my hair behind my ear. "You promised you'd make me cum without touching my clit or letting me touch her myself."

He nodded.

"That *could* hurt me," I said.

He slid his thumb into the waistband of his boxers.

My clit pulsated.

"Care to find out?" he asked.

CHAPTER 34

Grady slid off his underwear.

I gazed at his wonderful nude form.

"Your nipples are so erect, baby," he whispered, taking hold of his gargantuan cock. "I want to suck on them."

I rubbed my growing clitty through the outside of my negligee. "I love watching how you pleasure yourself," I said, moving slowly towards the bed as his hand moved on his member.

He took the cue, beginning to gently masturbate.

I leaned my chest forward.

Grady took down the lace front of my outfit and slipped one of my nipples between his lips.

I cradled his head.

He lovingly licked at my teat.

I moaned, roaming my fingernails through his hair.

He flicked his tongue around my nipple.

I kissed the side of his forehead.

He continued to funnel his fist up and down his phallus, as he grunted into my chest. He quickly swapped from one breast to the other, his free hand moving mine away from my crotch. Grady slid his fingers over the red lace around my she-balls, lightly patting them.

"You're amazing," I said quietly.

He pressed his palm into them, while sliding his middle-finger up to my rear.

I loved it the moment I felt his presence against my tight, little rosebud.

He clenched my nipple.

I let out a suppressed gasp.

He pushed the material of my thong-shaped bodysuit against my hole.

"I want to feel you there." I slapped my hand under his on the base of his cock. "I want to feel *this* there."

He let go of it.

I started to jerk him, enjoying the wealth of his warmth.

He seized hold of my other nipple with his free hand, carefully tweaking, while gently massaging the outermost edges of my anus.

I loved how sensual he was being and mimicked his speed with slow, tight up-and-down grasping movements of his rod. I kissed his head again, then dragged my nails down to his neck.

Grady flicked his fingers into the gusset of my bodysuit and swept it to one side, freeing my clit and my testes. He let them dangle, returning his attention to my rear. He rubbed several fingers all around my entrance, daring to almost touch it, then to caress the edges.

I could feel my heat grow tremendously within. I wanted this man inside me. I didn't care how rough things got between us. If there was even a chance he could make me orgasm from penetration alone I needed to know.

He grunted as my hand flew unintentionally faster up and down him.

"I love what you've made me, Grady."

He sucked harder on one nipple, twisting the other.

I selfishly shook my hips, hoping he'd notice my erection slap from one thigh to the other and take hold of her. I knew his promise, but I also knew he wasn't inside me yet. Surely a little hand-job wouldn't be a cardinal sin?

Grady released my teat, then ran his hand down the front of my negligee and grabbed my clitty. "She makes you a greedy girl, Maxine."

I nodded.

He tightened his grip, just holding her still. His middle-finger covered the whole of my hole.

My breathing was ragged.

His touch was magnificent.

"Oh my God, Grady, is this how you do it? Do you bring me to the brink of orgasm then fuck me?"

He grinned. "Not at all, angel."

I was cascading back and forth to meet his motions at my rear and at my front. "You must!"

"No, baby."

I hauled my negligee down to my belly, and squeezed his cock for dear life.

"Come here," he said, and swept me up in his arms. He pulled me down on the bed, sitting cowgirl atop his thighs. "Take hold of us both." He gestured to my clit and his cock. "Rub us together."

I knew I'd need both hands, and quickly. I took immediate hold of both our sexes, standing them up straight against each other. I started to wank us in unison. I was trying to greedily ground my ass into something.

Grady realised, and raised his knees, propping me up in mid-air.

"You're cruel," I whispered.

"I love you," he said.

I almost paused my hands.

"I love you too," I said finally, seconds after the shock of his statement began to sink in.

The demonic look in his eyes suggested otherwise, as his huge shaft throbbed against my inferior clitty.

"Thank you, Grady, thank you, thank you, thank you."

His fatty balls slapped up against my tiny she-ones.

"Because of you, I finally know who I am." I tried to shift myself forward, hoping to feel just something of his scrotum against my aching hole.

"And who's that, angel?"

"I'm Maxine. I'm a girl." I was rushing my hands up and down us. "I want to live like Maxine."

"Here?" he asked, his face flushing red. "With me?"

I couldn't bring myself to answer him.

Grady pulled my head to his, opening his mouth and entwining my tongue with his own.

I felt my heart flutter. I didn't want it to. I didn't need feelings for my dream psycho-cum-sweet-alpha-male.

His cock was so rugged against the softness of my clit.

I lost myself in my lust for his mouth, licking his lips and sucking down his saliva. He massaged the underside of my tongue. I groaned, my desires multiplying across many different levels. I humped his cock between my palms.

Grady tried to hide his laughter.

I bit his lip.

He grunted.

I parted my mouth from his, gazed into his eyes and hoped he knew what I wanted-

Grady grabbed my wrists, then pulled them away from our

genitals. "It's time, angel," he said, then leaned back and reached into his beside drawer. He pulled out a condom, ripped off the wrapping and swiftly sheathed his shaft.

"What position do you want me in?"

"*All* of them." He lifted me under my arms, then held me, facing him, over his crotch, with my asshole aiming downwards. "But we'll start with..."

"This," he said, and lowered my rectum onto the purple head of his cock.

My sphincter naturally resisted. "I need more foreplay."

He shook his head. "You do not, Maxine."

I wheezed.

He tried to let my weight take me down.

My anus refused him. "I do, Grady, I-"

He shushed me. "Trust me."

I locked my eyes with his.

"Trust me."

I reluctantly nodded.

Grady guided my lithe body downwards.

Precum glistened on my clit, as the entrance to my hole strived to stretch around his member. "Oh my God, Grady... You're so big."

He was pushing upwards.

"The biggest I've ever-"

He entered only perhaps an inch or so inside me.

It felt like more. My fingernails scratched at his shoulders. My clit bobbed in mid-air. "Oh, Grady, be careful."

"I will, angel," he said, and rubbed his thumbs into my flesh. "I promise."

I took a moment to regulate my breathing.

"You okay?" He throbbed beneath me. "You feel incredible."

"Yes." I tried to ease myself down more.

The grin on Grady's face was all the encouragement I needed.

My she-pussy was sore as she struggled to take the last of his great head. I ran my hands to his chest, distracting myself with anything I could reach for.

He popped all the way inside.

We smiled in unison.

"Baby," he cooed.

I showed him what this sissy was truly made of, forcing myself further down on him.

Shock and awe struck his sweet, handsome face.

I had to shut my eyes as the intensity soared beyond my safety boundaries. My nails dug into his skin. "Oh, Grady, you're *huge*... But you belong there." I'd never been so erect in my entire life. "Is this how you do it?" I looked down at my clit.

"No."

I clenched my internal muscles on his member.

He groaned.

My prostate was performing cartwheels.

Grady stroked my bare belly. "You were born to be a girl, Maxine."

"*Your* girl," I said, immediately fearing the consequences of leading him along. I couldn't help it. I knew what I wanted in my heart. Even in my head. And especially in my ass.

He struck himself higher.

I wheezed, my eyes rolling back in my head.

He slid himself down.

The sensation was extraordinary, at once threatening agony and inflicting pleasure. I seized hold of his chest hair. "Don't you dare drop out of me!"

He stabbed himself higher again.

"Fuck!" I wailed, my little body almost falling off the bed.

Grady steadied me by my side. "I've got you. I've *always* got you." He slapped the underside of my slit.

She pinged back into an upright position. I felt myself slide further down him. "Oh my God, Grady." My asshole felt red raw the deeper I took him. I didn't even know I had these depths!

He slapped the top of my clit.

She pinged back again. "How do you know these things?" I said, exasperated by excitement and disbelief.

Grady grabbed hold of my clit, masturbating her.

I sank further down his shaft to his base. I wailed, as I felt the warmth of his bloated balls beneath my buttocks.

His motions on my sex encouraged me to rock back and forth on him. He eased himself upwards, raising my body on his rod.

I felt such a sharp piercing inside, yet the manipulation he controlled on my clitty ensured I rode the waves which followed.

He returned his groin to the mattress, then powered up inside me again.

My chest heaved. I wheezed. Then smiled. "Yes, Grady, that's it. I can take it."

He gave my sex a final stroke and a squeeze. Then he let her loose.

I leaned myself forward, striving – and failing – to rub her on his stomach. "You're not going to let me touch myself, are you?"

"No."

I narrowed my eyes on his.

Grady flung his hips faster, driving his dick forcefully in and out of my asshole.

My palms fell to the bed, gripping the sheets. "Oh fuck! Oh fuck! Oh fuck!"

He lovingly stroked the sides of my stomach to my ribs.

I leaned my lips towards his.

He met them for the most incredible kiss. His pace maintained, drilling in and out of my hole.

I could take it. It wasn't brutal. It wasn't agonising. It was, actually, quickly becoming heavenly. I licked the entire circumference of his tongue.

Grady returned my affection with sensual swirls of his own.

My rear stretched adoringly around his girth. I was beginning to meet his strokes with thrusts of my own. I knew what was happening. Not that it'd happened often to me before. He wasn't fucking me – not yet, at least. He was making love to me. We were making love together.

"I mean it, angel," he said, tonguing saliva from my lips. "I love you."

"I love you too," I confessed, and no part of me felt I was being deceitful.

His palms roamed to my rear, pulling my cheeks apart.

I lost myself in the intensity, arching my back to meet his strokes.

Grady grunted, his face all smiles.

I gyrated my she-pussy on his cock. "You feel so right."

He tenderly kissed my lips, yet surrendered none of his rhythm.

I had my legs spread wide over his hips, my slit glistening with precum. Was it really actually possible he could make me cum like this?

He took hold of my head in both his hands, kissed me even deeper and plunged himself to the hilt up inside me.

My eyes bloated.

Trust me.

Grady leaned to his left, raising his right hip, and took both our bodies onto our sides.

My rectum ringed with a chorus of disdain and delight.

He began to fuck me with one of my legs pinned beneath him on the bed and the other raised high in the air.

My she-balls bounced with every strike, while my clit cried out for attention. She received none, yet still she stayed hard. "Yes, Grady!" I felt her pulsate like never before. "I can't believe how deep you're going."

He stroked my hair from my face, then looked me deep in my eyes.

I felt his every thrust career from my abdomen to my chest, and in particular matching every beat in my heart. "I'm glad I stayed."

He powered his penis home inside me.

I clung onto his shoulders, adoring the intensity.

"This isn't me *fucking* you," he said.

"I know, Grady." I smiled. "I know."

He started to tweak my nipples again. His balls slapped up against mine. His rod pummelled my tight, little hole, stretching her like no other before him.

I wanted so badly to touch my clitty.

His eyes suggested he read my mind, forbidding me.

I felt his cock strike my prostate again and again, only strengthening the state of my she-shaft.

"You're so beautiful," he said, and kissed me again.

I wrapped my leg in the air around his back, dragging him deeper inside me. It felt heavenly. I knew I could take him for as long as he wanted. My ass was his. I could sacrifice any amount of pain afterwards for his pleasure, yet in reality I felt significantly less pain than I'd anticipated.

His girth stretched my opening as he pulsated.

I hungrily kissed him back. I needed this. I needed him.

He wrapped my body up against his, trapping my clit between his stomach and mine.

I gyrated my hips, massaging my she-member with both our flesh.

"I can't get enough of you," he rasped, his hands roaming all over me. "You're perfect, baby." He pawed at my ass cheeks, sliding himself wonderfully in and out of me.

I rubbed my sex between us with more vigour. "I want to cum, Grady."

"You won't."

"I won't?" I demanded. "But I'm desperate! You promised you'd make me!"

He removed my leg from around his waist, caressing my skin as he did so. "I want to take you from behind."

Grady cupped my she-balls from behind me. "They're so cute and full, Maxine." His palm dwarfed them in size.

I was on all fours on the bed before him, my she-pussy empty and aching to be taken.

"Lean your head down on the bed, baby, and stick your ass up in the air."

I did as I was told.

Grady released a slight whistle.

I looked back at him, feeling incredibly vulnerable under his stare.

"I feel like I've waited my whole life for this... For *you*." He ran one hand over my ass. "Your skin is so soft. Your shape so round. You were built for this. Maxine, it's like somebody looked inside my head, saw everything I ever wanted in a *gurl*, and created you in that image."

I purred, then took my fingers to my negligee and slipped it over my rear, down my legs and off my body. I was naked. "Take me, Grady. Make love to me. I want you to cum."

He raised himself above my rump, pointed his cock at my hole and pressed it against the entrance.

My sphincter resisted, momentarily, then hungrily accepted his every inch. "Shit!" I gasped. "Oh my God, that's so good. So good, Grady."

He took hold of my tiny waist, then started to pump himself in and out of me.

I was moaning with delight.

Grady was grunting.

I flung my hands back to his thighs, lovingly stroking them. "You feel so good inside me."

"You feel amazing," he croaked.

I felt him ram faster, pillaging my body for his animal-like needs.

He flung his torso on top of my back, then tenderly kissed and licked from one upper arm, across my shoulder and back to the other arm. He was so endearing, while still striking my rectum with stroke after stroke after stroke.

My clit stayed hard, yet denied any physical contact at all. "I'm not going to cum like this," I cried.

"Not like this," he said, as if suppressing laughter at my predicament. "Maybe not even today."

"But Grady you promised me." I was slamming my ass back on his cock, anger driving my desire. "You promised you'd fuck me until you made me cum."

He kissed and nibbled on my neck, sending me into overdrive. "This isn't how I'd fuck you, angel."

"How would you fuck me?!?"

He swept my hair from my neck, then kissed me all over it again. "Another time."

Another time?!? But we wouldn't have another time. I was going home after he-

Grady stabbed my anus harder.

My eyelids rolled forward. "Oh my God, you're incredible!" An incredible fucker! But incredible is still what he was. "You fucking own me, Grady!"

He was getting ever faster, even licking from my neck to my jaw in swifter motions.

I fought desperately for his tongue with my own. "I want to kiss you!" I squealed.

His balls battered off my inner thighs. He shoved his lips to mine.

I struggled to kiss him properly back.

Grady dug his hands in above my hips, riding me harder.

I knew this was love. It was intense. And he was unquestionably fucking me hard now. But it wasn't going to make me cum. "I want to cum." I broke one hand free and started to slip it between my legs.

"I need to."

"No!"

I steadied it mere inches from my clit.

"Not like that, Maxine!"

My body was forced onto another plane, as he pummelled my ring with renewed vigour.

I succumbed to the weightless in my legs and collapsed on the bed, crushing my clitty below.

Grady came down atop me, riding my tightening anus hard. "Yes," he snarled. "Your she-pussy was made for this! I'm close, baby. I'm so very, very fucking close."

My body was beginning to tremble. Was this it? Was this my orgasm actually about to happen?

He struck himself up and down on me, as if performing push-ups.

I was pinned down by every downward stroke, my hands seizing the bed sheet.

"Yes!"

My anus squelched around his condom.

"I'm almost there, angel!"

I felt his sweaty chest on my back. "Cum in me, Grady!"

His behemoth rocketed up my rectum, vibrating me in places I'd never known to exist.

My innards were sending every shock wave to my trapped clitty. She was leaking so much precum. I believed him. I believed it was possible. I just needed him to last just a little bit longer-

Grady roared aloud, angrily gripping my flesh as if he wanted to tear me in two. His balls bounced against my anus. He pulsated inside. "Fuck! Yes!" He started to spurt between the walls of my ass, whilst still rocking his entire girth back and forth.

I dribbled onto the sheets.

He clamped his teeth on my neck.

I yelled out, exasperated by pain.

He was sucking hard on my skin.

"Oh, Grady, how can..." I live without this?

He rammed himself to the hilt inside me, his body convulsed several times over as he held his groin still, until his climax came to a slow, sensual stop. His mouth rested on my neck. His hands stroked the skin of my sides.

"That was amazing," I whispered.

"Yes, baby."

But I hadn't achieved orgasm.

"I know," he said. "I know what you're thinking. But you can't, Maxine."

"I can't?"

"You can't leave until I make you cum through penetration alone."

CHAPTER 35

I took my phone off the charger. The battery was full.

Grady was watching me like a hawk.

I had to decide. And swiftly.

"You're welcome to stay like that all day," he said, giving a little laugh as he gestured at my nudity.

I wasn't certain I would be staying all day. I needed to choose between my going home, male clothes or one of the wonderful outfits back in the bedroom.

"What is it, baby?" He came up behind me, slid his arms around me and pulled me against his clothed body. "You don't believe it's possible?"

My head was spinning. I knew I should text Jenny.

He kissed my shoulder. "I never expected you to cum when I made love to you. Not like that. Not the first time."

I could feel that bulge of his growing again against my ass already.

"But I *do* know how it'll happen... How I'll *make* it happen."

I set down my mobile, then turned around. His sex-on-legs manliness, from the glint in his eye to the broadness in his shoulders, melted my every resolve. "It was amazing, Grady-"

"But it was too sweet for you to achieve orgasm." He stared at my erect nipples. "There's only one true way to take you there to that level, angel."

I swallowed. "How?"

"You're a born subordinate... Fuck pig."

I was on the kitchen floor, as per his degrading instructions, applying my make-up with only a handheld mirror for assistance.

Grady was changing light bulbs in the ceiling overhead, barely giving me a second glance.

I felt humiliated. I felt taken for granted. I felt like my wishes to return home weren't even taken into consideration.

My mobile vibrated on the kitchen bench.

I felt like I wasn't allowed even to check it.

Grady whistled.

I felt like my clit would never go soft again.

"Very good," he said, not even looking at me.

I was stood naked below him, at the foot of his ladders, having presented myself for inspection.

"Pass me up a bulb, Maxine."

I reluctantly obeyed him.

"Cheers."

Cheers? What was I, some kind of drinking buddy?

He screwed the bulb into place. "I'll be with you in just a second." He passed me down the old one.

I didn't know what to do with it, but set it over beside my phone regardless.

"Then I'll pick you out something to wear."

He would? My heart sang.

"I've already got something in mind."

I saw Jenny's text. She was asking if I could pick her up in the morning.

"Something which just screams... Fuck pig."

I looked up to him.

Grady was looking at me. He had a demonic smile on his face.

I unlocked my phone. I typed out a message.

"Who you texting?" he asked, setting his work boots one at a time down each rung of the ladder.

"My sister," I answered.

"Why, what're you saying?"

I recognised that wavering, unattractive tone his in voice I'd little to no time for. That hint of vulnerability I could seek no solace within.

"Maxine!"

I hit send, then set the phone down. "I told her I can't pick her up in the morning."

He stepped onto the floor. "Good girl." He clicked his fingers. "Follow me."

Grady's eyes wouldn't leave my body, as I sat naked on the bed and prepared to dress in what he'd chosen.

"You *are* so very beautiful, baby," he said. "You can keep that in the back of your mind, if you need to. You know how I feel about you."

I looked up to him. Maybe I needed to hear it again.

"But there's more than one way I like to treat you."

I looked down, as I slipped one leg into a black, knee-high, fuck-me boot.

"Are you listening to me, fuck pig?"

"Yes, sir."

"Good girl."

I zipped up the second boot, then set my feet down and stood to familiarise myself with the feel of the ridiculously high platform heels.

"You look hot," he said. "But can you walk on them?"

I doubted I'd be doing much walking, although I tried to appease him nonetheless and took myself on a little march around the bedroom.

Grady frustrated me when he didn't even reach out to fondle my clitty when I passed him both times.

"Seems doable," I said, then sat back down on the bed. "What else do you want me to wear for you, sir?"

"Just these."

I watched him go to the wardrobe. I knew what implements were inside.

He didn't crouch to retrieve the box, and instead searched up high, higher than I could reach.

My jaw dropped as he turned to reveal a leather collar and chain.

"These are befitting of a fuck pig, don't you agree?"

I thought I was too much in awe to answer, yet subconsciously I'd already started to nod.

"Good girl."

I started to stand.

"Something tells me you're going to do whatever I tell you to today... Fuck pig."

I raised my head to give him full access to my neck. "Yes, sir."

CHAPTER 36

Grady smacked my bare cheeks, stinging both the exterior flesh and the innards still aching from his earlier love-making. "Hurry up, sissy!"

I was cooking as fast as I could.

"It's late enough as it is already. She'll be getting hungry *and* agitated. I don't want her worrying that something's wrong."

"Yes, Grady," I said, knowing better than to question anything regarding his mother.

He pinched hold of one buttock. "Are you being cheeky with me?" he demanded.

I shook my head.

He yanked the leash, trailing my neck to one side. "Answer me when I speak to you, fuck pig."

My clit swiped precum on the front of the oven door beneath the hob. I hoped he wouldn't notice. "No, sir, I'm not being cheeky with you. I never would. I live to honour and serve you. On hand and foot... On hands and knees too."

He slackened the chain. "Good girl."

I could see there was a message from Jenny on my phone.

He inhaled. "It smells ready. Why isn't it ready?"

"It's *almost* ready, Grady. I promise. I just want to make it perfect for..."

He raised one eyebrow.

I didn't dare finish the sentence.

"Yes," he said. "That's what I thought, fuck pig." He strode off into the living room.

I quickly leaned to my phone.

"What about these?"

I stood up straight, ignoring my mobile.

He was holding up my male clothes. "Can I burn these yet?"

Oh fuck.

"Well, fuck pig?"

I didn't know what to say. Or, rather, how to say it.

"You're fucking useless sometimes, Maxine." He threw them behind the sofa. "Always a cock-tease. Never cock-hungry enough."

"I am cock-hungry," I whined, high-pitched.

Grady looked out the window. "It looks cold out."

I reached for my phone.

"I hope you're ready to brave the elements."

Brave the elements? What'd he have planned?

"Mother's food won't take itself up."

I read Jenny's reply. She was demanding to know why I couldn't pick her up. Was something wrong? Was her car okay?

"Fuck pig!" he snapped.

I lifted the pot off the hob. "It's coming now." I scooped the contents onto a plate, then wrapped it in cellophane to keep it warm. I wanted to ask him if she'd require extra salt, but again thought better of making any reference to her at all.

He laughed as he watched me.

"What's so funny?" I said.

"Her." He pointed. "She's still hard."

I ignored him.

"Come on." He took hold of the leash again, and began to lead me out of the kitchen. "You can carry that up to her cottage. I'll lead the way... We'll see if your little clitty stays hard out in the elements."

The crunch of the platforms of my boots echoed up and down the lane as I walked behind Grady, led forcefully by the leash in his hand.

I looked beyond the foliage. "They could be watching me."

"Who?"

"Dominic... And Nick."

"You'd love that, fuck pig."

"No, I wouldn't!"

He tutted.

I carried his mother's lunch in silence behind him.

He kept looking over his shoulder at my clit.

A cool breeze made me shiver.

"She's fading," he remarked, jerking at the leash to hurry me up.

I waited until he looked forward again, then quietly jerked her to try to keep her hard. I had to be so careful not to drop his mother's meal. But it felt so good to touch myself. I just-

He looked.

I froze.

He stopped walking.

So did I.

"You're cheating?" he snapped.

I was lost for words.

"Get your hand off her!"

I released my sex. "Grady, I'm sorry-"

"Shut up, fuck pig!"

A greater gust of wind blew over the hedges and between the trees.

I was so suddenly cold.

Grady tugged at the leash, guiding me closer to him.

I took tentative steps.

"I was going to bring you up to mother's house," he said. "I was going to introduce you as my girlfriend."

Like this? Completely naked but for my boots, collar and leash. He had to be kidding!

"See if she approved of my choice." He locked his eyes on my clit.

I said nothing.

He stared at her as the cold winds slowly but surely softened her.

My heart was beating so fast. My blood was rushing all away from my she-shaft. I wanted desperately to keep my erection.

"You lost it, fuck pig."

I wanted to protest how it was still semi-

"And you jerked off without permission." He tugged the chain until I was right up against him. "Do you want me to kiss you?"

I reluctantly nodded.

He licked my cheek instead. "Tough, sissy. You'll not be meeting mother today. You're too disobedient. Not subservient enough. Not a proper fuck pig."

"I will be a proper fuck pig, sir." Why was I protesting? "I promise." I didn't want him to give in and take me into his mother's cottage in this state of undress. "Please."

"You need punished," he said, and slipped the leash out of his grip.

I cowered, waiting for him to whip me with it.

Grady looked up. "Just the thing," he said, then stretched high on his tiptoes, so he could slide the leash onto a vertical branch well out of my reach. He made sure to place it so no amount of pulling from me on the ground could disrupt it. "You'll wait here, alone, dressed like that until I come back."

I bit my lip to silence my disagreement.

"I don't care who you hear coming, fuck pig, you'll make no effort to hide."

I gulped.

He checked the restraint on my collar. "You're safely locked in."

I'd little doubt otherwise.

Grady grabbed the plate from me. "I guess I'll tell her *I* made this since you're such a fucking disappointment."

My clitty bobbed up due to his insult.

He shook his head. "Such a fuck pig."

I watched in disbelief as he turned to walk up the lane towards his mother's without me.

"Just say it," Grady barked back at me. "I can read you like a book, sissy."

I hesitated. "Please don't be long."

He laughed. "If you see Nick, try to restrain yourself." He laughed louder. "Restrain!?! Oh, fuck pig, sometimes I even amuse myself... *Restrain*."

CHAPTER 37

I made it at least two minutes since Grady had disappeared out of sight before I tried to drag the leash off the branch. I yanked at the chain. I tried to fling it upwards. Anything just to get the leash to budge. It wouldn't work. The branch pointed to the sky. Even on my ridiculous platform heels I didn't have the height necessary to lift it down.

I was literally stuck here, my collar locked in place around my throat.

Wind struck my clit.

What if Dominic or his son Nick were hanging around? I'd already caught Nick spying on me through the bedroom window once already. I thought about it for a second. He was a tall lad. If I told him I was here like this against my will would he free me?

My fucking clitty was hard as a rock again, as if the futility of my very predicament somehow excited me.

It did.

And I needed to break free from more than the physical chain holding me in place.

I looked up the lane again.

There was no sign of Grady.

I glanced to the chain running from my neck to the branch.

My arousal had me rooted to Grady just as much as this bondage.

I grabbed hold of my clit and started to masturbate her furiously.

Birds took off immediately out of the tree.

I pounded my she-shaft in my fist.

There was still remnants of frost in the fields.

I flung my foreskin back and forth.

This was essential. He'd invaded my head, never mind my heart and my hole, and my desire to cum was more than just a selfish need. I needed to regain my resolve and get the fuck away from him before nightfall.

I could still get the car back in time to pick Jenny up. I could still find a moment to text her and reassure her I'd got mixed up somehow and that I could pick her up from the airport after all.

My mind became convoluted with images of Grady's muscular body. Of vivid memories of him taking me in my ass. I loved it. I literally loved it. I just needed to climax my way out of this hold he had on me.

Anyone could be watching me masturbate my naked body.

I felt my rousing intensify.

Even Grady could be secretly watching. He knew these parts better than anyone.

I knew he'd punish me even more severely if he caught me.

He'd possibly leave me out here all day... Or all night.

I felt heat surge within my chest.

How long had I been stood like a slut like this? Mere minutes, surely? But it was so easy to lose track of time when I was so vigorously pumping my sex. It could've been longer than I realised. He could already have given the lunch to his mother. He could've made his small talk with her. There was every chance he was already on his way back down the lane.

My she-balls were bulging, and I massaged them with my free hand.

I tried to focus on my freedom.

It was no use. My head warred between rebellion and subservience. I wanted him to catch me. To strictly admonish me. Then to take me. Hard. With pure anger.

Like a fuck pig should be taken.

I grunted in the most unladylike of fashions. I couldn't care enough to prevent myself from doing it again and again as I lost myself in my lust.

A breeze blew a whiff of my own perfume across my nostrils.

I felt the collar catch at my throat as I rocked back, flicking my wrist faster on my she-phallus.

There was still no Grady on the lane.

I knew he'd be close. I either gave up now or I ploughed on to my climax.

I hesitated.

I fucked my own hand, as if my lust overpowered my hips against the doubts in my mind.

I could still feel him where he'd made love to me that morning. I knew I wanted more. I needed more.

Cum and then run.

Only Grady could free me from the tree.

Cum, play possum, then run.

I almost cried out as I felt my orgasm rush closer. I desperately needed this. My release would be my everything.

My sphincter pulsated, as if demanding someone – or something – penetrate it at once.

I looked up the lane.

I hammered my tiny sex.

I looked up again.

I felt a rush of blood to my head. I saw stars. I needed to fucking cum!

I was breathless as I regained my composure. I looked down at my cum on the grass verge at the side of the lane.

What the fuck had I done?

I saw my she-semen stuck to my hand.

What the fuck had I done?

I skipped quickly to the verge like a typical effeminate sissy and rubbed my hand on old leaves.

There was still no sign of Grady.

I stood up again.

Shit! There he was! He was walking at pace towards me!

I stood with one leg in front of the other, then felt cum at my thigh. I couldn't wipe it without him seeing me do so. Fuck, what if he smelt it?

I had to get away from him.

Yes.

It was true now. I felt it again. My mind was clear again. I'd orgasmed and my intentions were back on track, just as I'd planned.

He wasn't carrying his mother's plate.

I had to leave.

He looked pissed off.

Or was that just my imagination?

He certainly looked intense.

I looked away from him for just a moment, scouring the horizon for signs of anyone else.

"Well, well, well, fuck pig, look at you all alone," he said.

I peeled my eyes from the tiny, girly amount of love juice I'd forgotten to hide in the grass.

"Did you behave yourself while I was away?"

"Yes, sir," I said, and even I felt I heard something in my voice less-than-subtly suggest I was feigning obedience.

Grady scoured the surrounding area. "Was Nick here?"

"Of course he wasn't, Grady." I gestured to the leash on the branch. "Please, will you lift that down?"

He walked around me. "I have to inspect you first, fuck pig. Make sure you're not lying to me about Nick."

"I'm not, sir."

He cleared his throat.

I could smell cigarette smoke from him.

"Dominic doesn't realise his son is that way inclined." Grady put his hand on my ass. "Y'know, that he'd give his right ball for a crack at this."

I doubted that was true.

"I sincerely hope you didn't lead him astray with this fuck pig asshole of yours."

I tried to avert my eyes from my love juice.

He pulled my cheeks apart to inspect my rectum. "It seems you're telling the truth, Maxine." Grady walked around to the front of me. "I'm pleasantly surprised."

I knew my clit was glistening with cum.

"It seems I've trained you well, after all," he said, and stroked my face.

"Thank you, sir."

He looked down my chest, then further-

"Grady."

He glanced up to my lips. "Yes?"

"Please can you take the leash down from the tree?"

He grinned. "Fuck, you're so beautiful... For a fuck pig." He turned to the tree, stretched and retrieved the leash.

"Thank you-"

He jerked my neck towards him.

I stumbled just a couple of steps.

"I bet you're so frustrated you can't wait for another fucking," he said.

I felt a fire within. I wasn't frustrated at all. Not sexually. I had to restrain my willingness to defy him, and thought quickly – too quickly – to change the subject. "Where's the plate?" I asked innocently.

"Up there."

"Did your mother enjoy the lunch I made her?"

His eyes changed to a fierce, destructive stare.

Oh fuck. My heart sank. I'd broken the cardinal rule. I'd mentioned her. "Sir, I wasn't thinking. I didn't mean anything-"

CHAPTER 38

He slammed the front door behind us.

"Grady, I'm sorry. I didn't mean anything by it. I didn't mean to mention her like that. I was just concerned, hoping my cooking was okay."

His silence frightened me more than anything.

I looked to my phone.

"You want to leave?" he snapped.

I shook my head.

"Then go to the bedroom."

Text Jenny.

"What is it, fuck pig?"

I hesitated, wondering if I should ask him for permission to reply to my sister's last text? The one where she'd seemed more concerned about her car than me.

"You have something to ask me? Go ahead."

I backed up from him, gradually taking myself towards the hall to the bedroom.

"You want to know if there's a particular reason I don't want you to mention my mother?"

I shook my head.

"There is, Maxine. But that's no business for a fuck pig."

I looked down.

"Go to the bedroom. Lift out the box of tricks from the wardrobe. You know which one. Then lie on the bed. Do it, fuck pig. Now."

I wasn't remotely turned on by the way he was speaking to me. Not anymore.

"Move it, fuck pig!" he bellowed.

"Remember, *you* wanted me to treat you like a fuck pig," Grady said, entering the bedroom. "You know you need it." He looked at my crossed legs. "It's the only way you'll get off."

I lay on my back on the bed. Had I wanted it though? I certainly couldn't remembering asking him to treat me like this.

He set his hands on the box beside me. "Spread your legs,

angel."

I reluctantly obeyed him.

"Good girl."

My resolve would not be melted.

He slid the lid off.

I swallowed, playing down the sensation the mere sound of it caused within my sphincter.

Grady looked in the box.

I was briefly relieved he was no longer surveying my sex. I hadn't been able to get to the bathroom to clean away the evidence of my wank.

He was grinning. "There's so many things in here befitting a fuck pig," he said.

I wondered if I could settle for fuck queen.

Grady lifted out a dildo of similar size to his cock. "But I think we'll just start with this." He set it down on my crotch, dwarfing my clitty. "What do you say to that?"

"Yes, sir."

"Good girl."

My clit was so shrivelled and spent.

"Take the dildo, Maxine. It's big and black. Take it and wet it with your mouth."

I was almost trembling as I took hold of it. I told myself to find my nerve. I knew Grady. I practically trusted him. He could play a fantasy out. But he was vulnerable in his own ways too. I had the true power here. I had the ability to just stand up and walk out the door... Never to return.

"Good girl," he said, rubbing his cock through his jeans as he watched me slide the dildo deep into my mouth.

I deep-throated it.

Lust lit up his eyes.

I chastised myself for almost enjoying my tease, as I slurped at the fake member, my hands returning to my crotch only to shield my sex from any inspection.

"That's it, angel, suck it down good."

I diligently gave it great oral sex. I knew if it was a real man's cock the guy would be grunting already. I could really suck cock. I knew it. Grady knew it. Every man who'd ever had the privilege knew it.

Grady unzipped his jeans, then pulled out his erection.

I averted my eyes from it.

"You playing hard to get, slut?"

I was doing more than playing, and let my gaze stray to the bedroom window.

"Don't pretend you want to leave again... Not before you've shot your load."

Been there. Done that.

Grady walked around the bed to block my view. "Tell me you want this," he said, pulling on his member.

I sucked the dildo so hard and fast I made it impossible to answer.

"So be it." He seized the leash, stretching the chain to my collar. "Roll over onto your front."

I clenched the sex toy with my teeth, then flipped onto all fours.

"Spit it out, fuck pig."

I sent the dildo careering forward onto our pillows.

Ours?

Grady grabbed it. "Time to warm that ass pussy of yours up again," he said.

You've no intention of walking out of here.

He jumped up on the bed.

No intention of picking your sister up from the hospital.

He came up behind me.

No intention of even texting her back again.

Grady positioned the huge head of the dildo at my hole. "Ready?"

Ever.

I ignored him.

He yanked the leash, straining my neck back. "Ready, fuck pig?"

"Yes, sir," I said, through gritted teeth, as I spilled saliva.

"Let's see what you're fucking made of then." He pushed the dildo into my asshole. "Oh yes, baby's ripe for a milking today."

I was seething. "I thought you said *you'd* fuck me to orgasm, not this dildo."

He jammed it deep up inside me. "I fucking will, fuck pig." He wrapped the chain around his knuckles, arching my back even more.

I couldn't control my grunts, as my lifeless clitty flopped around beneath me.

"I hear you, slut, grunting like the fuck pig you long to be."

I almost hated how I was beginning to mentally enjoy his disgusting tone towards me. Why did such disdain trigger an attraction to him inside me?

"You never mention my mother, do you hear me, fuck pig?" he snapped, roughly fucking the dildo in and out of my ass.

"Yes, sir."

"Who do you never mention, fuck pig?"

"I know who, sir."

"Then say who, you stupid sissy."

"I can't, sir."

"Why, fuck pig?"

"Because I'm forbidden."

He shoved the dildo all the way to its fake balls inside me. "Good girl."

My only solace in my despicable enjoyment was the flaccidity in my she-penis.

Grady dragged me by my collar onto my side, then onto my back. "Spread wide, fuck pig." He had a firm grip on the dildo, violently rifling it in and out of my fuckhole. "Oh, look at how limp she is." He laughed. "What's the matter? You only get erect for the real thing?"

I tried to fake an innocent nod.

"I don't believe you," he said, but his grin suggested he was a million miles from the truth.

I couldn't contain my grunts, as the dildo stretched my anus in ways different to how his cock had. It was the girth, I reasoned, somewhat thicker at the base than his.

He toyed with the leash, jerking my throat forward momentarily then slacking it.

I reached down to my buttocks, pulling them apart to allow the dildo all the way inside.

Grady's own cock visibly throbbed.

My clitty remained soft and spent.

"You're not a stupid, little girl. You engineered this, didn't you? You knew how I'd react when you mentioned her. You wanted me to lose my rag. You wanted me to take you in here and use things on you." He looked into the box. "So many things in here I could use to break you, baby."

My chest inflated with anxiety.

"But you don't want to be my baby, do you?"

I surrendered to a wavering nod.

He squeezed his girth. "You want to be my fuck pig." He twisted the dildo up inside me, in rotations no cock could ever possibly perform on me.

My eyes rolled back in my head. Oh my God, I was starting to want him again. I was supposed to know better than this.

You do know better.

Than I was supposed to do better.

You can do better.

I pushed my rear down on the dildo.

Grady shifted his knees under my thighs.

I was able to propel myself deeper down on the toy.

"Oh, fuck pig, you'll definitely start getting hard now."

If you don't, he'll know.

"I might even give you a little oral."

He'll work it out.

He steadied the dildo inside me. "In fact..." Grady leaned his lips down to my sex, then took all of her easily into his mouth.

I gasped, not through stimulation but through fear.

He tongued my slit. "I can taste precum already."

Except it wasn't precum.

"Tastes different."

He knows.

He sucked her to the base.

I felt him redouble his efforts with the dildo.

Don't you dare.

I was caught in a confusing mix of pleasure and distress. I was enjoying every second of the fake cock in my ass – loving it even – yet my desires to take myself off and away from him hadn't evaporated... Yet.

Grady licked around the circumference of my clit, then easily threw her around his mouth. At first, side-to-side. Then up and down.

I was somewhat numb, but not so much I couldn't tell she was still lifeless between his lips. My she-balls were so tiny and empty too.

He careered his mouth up and down her.

My rectum squelched around the dildo.

He tugged on the chain until I started to choke.

I squirmed in his mouth.

Grady hit the head of the dildo off my prostate.

My clitty still wouldn't react.

His frustration was becoming as obvious as the futility of trying.

I wasn't going to get erect, despite my growing enjoyment in my ass.

He growled along my limpness.

I wanted to get hard for him. I did. I could feel all my insides crave him again. What was wrong with me? Did I really need him that bad? Would I always need him? Was this the difference between needing and wanting? Even if I wanted not to need him, would I always need to have him in my-

Grady spat out my sex. "Something's wrong here," he said. "How the fuck do you expect to cum when you can't even get hard for me?"

I panicked. "Call me fuck pig."

He hesitated.

"Please, sir."

He lifted my petite length, then let her fall flat above my scrotum. "You've masturbated. I don't understand when or even where, but you have."

I froze.

"Deny it."

I couldn't.

You really ought to.

I wouldn't lie to this man.

Just wait to see what punishment he has in store for you now.

Maybe I wanted to be punished.

Degrading won't even be in it, fuck face.

A look of realisation dawned on his face. "You fucking didn't, did you?"

I tried to make my disobedience look dirty, deliberately feigning innocence with a meek look to one side.

"You jerked off while I was at my mother's!"

I felt the dildo begin to slide out of my hole, and tried desperately to seize it with the muscles of my sphincter.

"Why?" he demanded. "Why would you ruin this?"

I exhaled the most uneasy of breaths.

"You *do* want to leave." He yanked the chain until I was upright, then he jumped off the bed and dragged me onto the floor behind him.

The dildo dropped out of me.

"Then leave is what you'll fucking do!"

CHAPTER 39

Grady stormed through his cottage, dragging me behind him.

I was trying to get up off my knees, but he was pacing too fast for me to find my feet. "Grady, please! Don't be so rough!"

"Shut up, fuck pig!"

I was so pathetic I found joy in still being fuck pig.

He threw the leash down on the living room floor.

I suddenly lost the will to get off my knees.

He pounded into the kitchen. "Well, you can't leave without your possessions." He grabbed my mobile, then turned to the table and lifted my car keys.

I looked over to the sofa, where he'd earlier thrown my male clothes.

Grady strode right over to me, his knee almost clashing with my face.

I was looking at his cock, almost salivating. I'd have sucked it all afternoon if it would alter his mood. In fact, all night.

He stuffed it back in his jeans. "Take these," he said, shoving my phone and keys into my hands. Then he grabbed the leash and dragged me towards the front door.

I had to use my elbows and knees to walk on. "What about my-"

He silenced me with a stare.

Male clothes? I'd dared not finish my sentence aloud.

Grady opened the door. "Stand."

I got off my knees.

"Get out."

"Sir, please-"

Grady shoved me through the doorway.

I spun around in time to see him slam the door behind me. I immediately tried the handle. It'd locked itself.

He bolted it for added measure.

"Grady!" I yelled, my voice dispersing birds from nearby trees. "Grady!" I hit the door with my elbow. "Grady!" I went quickly to the window to the living room, and started whacking it. "Let me back in! I'm sorry, Grady!"

He didn't appear in the living room.

I went back to the front door and started to hit it again, knowing he was stood right behind it. My clitty was on show for anyone who cared to drop by. My erect nipples and bare ass too. "Grady, let me in!"

Silence fell as I stopped and he continued to ignore me.

I sat my ass down on the front step and crossed my legs. I set the leash of the chain in my lap. I felt at the collar around my neck. It was locked into place. I had the keys to Jenny's car in one hand. If I left now, this collar and my boots were all I had to wear for a drive back to the city.

The sun was shining.

It wouldn't be dark for a few hours yet.

I hit my elbow behind myself on the door.

Nothing.

I opened up my mobile and read my sister's last text again. Was something wrong, she'd asked, followed by is the car okay?

She cares more about the car than you.

I typed out Everything's wrong, then deleted the message.

CHAPTER 40

I waited on the doorstep for an hour. It felt longer. But I knew it was only an hour because of the time on my phone.

One whole hour and Grady hadn't appeared once to check on me.

I'd been watching the window non-stop and listening out for footsteps behind the door. Nothing. I didn't know whether he was still stood there or if he'd long since disappeared somewhere else in the cottage.

I stood up in my platform knee-high boots and stretched, the chain and leash dangling between my legs and catching my clitty.

I was outdoors, naked, yet somehow comfortable at being so in the warm sunlight. It could've been a liberating experience. My phone and car keys in hand too. Yet the collar and leash, and my clothes locked indoors, made it very, very clear I was still his prisoner.

I decided to take a walk around his home, starting in a clockwise direction. I looked in both the living room windows, but there was no sign of him. I walked on to the bathroom. No luck. I walked the opposite wall from the front of the house and turned again. I came up to the bedroom window and looked in. He wasn't there. He'd made the bed, though. And he'd tidied away the box of tricks I'd wished somehow to have used on me by now. I ventured on towards the kitchen, hoping I'd missed him move from room to room when I'd been away from a window.

Grady wasn't visible in the kitchen nor in the living room.

I rapped the window.

No answer.

I walked on around to the second window, looking down on the kitchen sink, and hit it with my knuckles.

Nothing.

I walked dejectedly onwards to the front door and slouched back down on the step.

Hope was evaporating. What if the game was over? What if Grady really did want me to just drive off?

I looked at Jenny's car. The so-called pink fuck mobile. I could get in it now. I could drive off. I'd never find my way back here. I'd no idea where in the hell I was. I'd be out of Grady's life forever.

It's what he wants. He wants a real *subservient fuck pig. Not a one wank wonder.*

I felt so unworthy of him.

I dared rub my little clit with my wrist. Just a bit. Just to make sure she was still alive.

The living room window swung open.

I jumped up.

"What are you still doing here?" he snapped.

I marched over to the window.

"Stop. That's close enough."

I froze a mere two feet from the window.

"I want you to leave, Maxine. I didn't throw you out to hang about outside. Go."

I thanked my lucky stars he didn't stop at Max. "Grady, I don't want to leave." Not without my clothes, at the very least. "I want to stay."

"No, you wanted to wank yourself off so you wouldn't be tempted to stay."

I shook my head. "I *can't* leave you, Grady."

"Why?" he asked, his tone mocking. "Because you're in love with me?"

I wouldn't insult his intelligence again. "No, sir, because you told me I can't leave until you make me cum through penetration alone." I tried to pass the leash through the window to him. "I want you to fuck the she-spunk out of me."

Grady tossed the leash back out. "You can't even get hard. Get the fuck outta here, sissy."

"No, Grady, it's fuck-"

He shut the window.

"Pig."

The sun was setting and my body was reacting to the change in temperature, shivering, my skin dotting in goosebumps as well.

I unlocked my mobile and went back to my sister's text. I typed out my reply, telling her I wouldn't be back.

I'd no idea what I'd do about her car.

I hit send.

She could make whatever of that she wished.

But I was as adamant as I was defiant – I would not be leaving my man!

I was so cold under the moonlight.

I checked the time. It was almost 9pm.

Grady had to be hungry by now. So why hadn't he demanded my presence to cook for him? Surely he hadn't made something himself?

I looked up the long driveway. What if a delivery driver suddenly appeared and I was sat here naked? Although somehow I doubted a country boy like Grady would ever order takeaways. And, besides, he'd no telephone... Or so he claimed.

I played with the car keys. Why didn't I just go sit in the car? I could start the engine, get the heat on and warm myself up. There was a chance the sound of the engine starting might even give Grady the kick up the ass he needed.

But I knew him. He'd be subtle. Even if he watched me, he'd make sure I wouldn't see him. He'd call my bluff within seconds.

Then why didn't I just move the car down the driveway? Even just out of sight?

I stood up to stretch my legs.

My heels scuffing stones were the only sounds in the night air.

"Fuck this," I said.

The front door opened behind me.

I spun around.

Grady stood there with his arms folded.

"Sir," I whispered. "Grady, please-"

"Why are you still here?"

"There's nowhere else I want to be." I walked towards him, more than expecting him to tell me to stop in my tracks. "Listen, take this." I held out my mobile to him. "I don't need it. I texted my sister. I told her I'm not coming back."

Grady took my phone.

I wanted to give him my leash too, but I didn't have the optimism to push my luck.

"You're still not hard," he said.

I grabbed my sex. "I'll make her hard for you, I promise."

"Let the fuck go of her now!"

I dropped her.

"No cheating, slut!"

Fuck, I could feel his existing anger amplify and resonate through his words into my soul.

"You will stay out here. You will *not* touch yourself. And if, and only *if*, you can make that little thing hard again, will I consider letting you back in. Do you understand?"

I nodded.

"Speak when you're spoken to!"

"Yes, sir, I understand." I took a nervous hold of the chain, accidentally caressing it against my clit.

Grady pointed at my face. "If you cheat, I'll know."

"I won't cheat, sir. I'll never disappoint you again. I won't leave you. Just please call me fuck pig. *Your* fuck pig. Please!"

"Slut," he said, and threw the door shut in my face.

CHAPTER 41

"Fuck pig," he said, smiling as he looked down at my length.

"How did you know?" I asked. I'd been staring at the living room window for the last five minutes. It was the only way he could've seen me. And he hadn't appeared.

"It doesn't matter." He reached for the leash, then gently pulled me towards him. "All that matters is... Have you learnt your lesson?"

"Yes, sir."

"Were you a stupid, little girl more than once today?"

I nodded profusely. "Very much so. I'm a ridiculous fuck pig."

He grinned. "Talk some more like that."

My erection seemed to stiffen. What the fuck was wrong with me that I found it such a turn-on to be demeaned by him? This man who I knew could make such sweet, tender love to me? "I'm a dumb, moronic, city slut, fuck pig. I'm completely incapable of outwitting you, Grady- I mean, sir, and I should never attempt to again."

He began to wrap the chain around my little girth. "More."

"I feel you in every part of me, sir. In my body and in my mind, even especially when you're absent. I live for you. I only want to be with you. I'm your fuck pig, and I'll stay out here completely naked all night if it'll please you."

"It would, angel."

I felt my heart rejoice. I was angel again! "I'll take off my boots and walk all over these hard stones in my bare feet."

His smile grew even wider.

"I'm just a stupid fuck pig... And I'll never be anything more."

He tightened the chain. "I'm going to cut off your blood supply."

My fears rose. "Yes, sir, anything you wish."

Grady grabbed the back of my head, then pulled my mouth to his.

Grady lay me down naked on his bed. "I'm sorry," he whispered.

"What?" I asked, my whole being dishevelled with disbelief.

"For being caught up in the whole fantasy of treating you like shit."

It was a fantasy?

"Maxine, I'm falling in love with you." He armed his brow. "The truth is... I'm terrified of losing you."

I breathed gently out over him. I wanted to tell him he wouldn't. I wanted to promise him he wouldn't.

"I act tough. I act hard. I act heartless even. And it's to push you a distance away. I know I've opened myself to a lot of hurt."

I blinked, letting my eyelids stay shut for just a second. "*I'm* sorry, Grady. I've confused you. I get muddled up too."

He kissed me again, then unlocked the collar from my neck. He looked so sad.

I slid my palm to his face. "Hey."

He kissed my fingers.

"It's okay, Grady. I *enjoy* being treated like that. Maybe we need to set up some boundaries, or come up with a safe word..."

He gave a slight chuckle.

"But I *do* enjoy it. I get off on you treating me like your fuck pig-"

"*A* fuck pig," he interrupted, smiling again. "It makes you sound so much sluttier."

I smiled too. "I can be as slutty as you want. I promise you I'll act loose and slutty, if it pleases you. But know one thing, Grady... Sir... I'm yours... And yours alone."

"Thank you, angel."

I wrapped my bare legs around his clothed torso. "I texted my sister. I didn't tell her where I am. She expected me to pick her up from the airport in the morning." I took a deep, deep breath, knowing my next sentence would change everything. "I told her I wasn't coming back."

"Ever, Maxine?"

"So, if you're planning to tie me up and murder me... No one will ever find me."

Grady gently dry humped my clitty. "I can promise to tie you up."

"And, let's say even if theoretically I were to change my mind, *you* have my phone. I don't want to know where you've hidden it. I want to be at your mercy. I love being controlled by you, Grady. I don't know why, because I never wanted this with anyone else, but I fucking adore being a slave to your lust."

"It's *love*, baby. Maybe a kind of fucked up love, but I love you."

I wanted to ask about his mother. To know why I couldn't mention her. Surely he should share that secret with the one he loved. "I love you too, Grady."

He rubbed my shoulders and sides. "You're so cold."

I nodded.

"Do you want to get under the duvet?"

"Please."

Grady rolled off me to one side.

I slid up and under the duvet, patting a spot beside me for him to join.

He duly obliged, unbuttoning his shirt and quickly discarding it.

I helped him out of his jeans and boxers.

Grady rampantly fucked my ass. He was facing me, the two of us entwined on our sides. His hands roamed my body. His tongue explored my mouth.

I was so turned on his as funnelled himself ever further into my rear.

His balls slapped at my ass.

I wanted to touch my clitty. She was so hard. I knew I could cum if he'd just let me play with her. Even a little.

He didn't offer.

I didn't ask.

"I love having sex with you," he said, stabbing me faster. "Especially in this position."

My legs were spread wide.

His sweat dripped from his forehead to my lips.

I licked it up. "I love every taste of you I can get," I said, my voice rumbling from a gargle to a grunt.

He drilled me so fucking hard.

My fingernails dragged into his flesh. "Don't you fucking dare stop, Grady!"

"I'm close," he rasped.

I needed to cum.

"So close, angel."

Why wasn't he calling me fuck pig?

He was roaring as he pinned me in place.

Why couldn't I bring myself to ask him to?

He fucked my hole so hard I thought he might split me.

To beg him to?

"Fuck!" Grady yelled, and ejaculated deep into the condom inside me.

I wrapped my legs around him, holding him in place, desperate not to let him slide out a moment too soon.

He continued to career in and out of me for several high-velocity strokes.

I could feel the warmth of his sperm through the rubber. I wasn't even sure if it was my imagination, but certainly I sensed a warmth inside me.

"I really fucking adore you," he said.

"I love you, Grady," I replied, knowing his passing orgasm would likely take with it the depth of his feelings.

"I *love* you, angel." He pulled me tight to him and kissed me hard.

My erect clit was trapped between us, literally throbbing, as his own hard on slowly softened. "Sleep inside me. If you can. I want you to stay in my she-pussy all night long."

He nodded.

"Promise you'll try?"

Grady's cock somehow pulsated in my rectum. "I won't have to try." He cradled my head on his shoulder. "This is exactly where I belong, baby."

I closed my eyes. I was fulfilled, yet frustrated. I'd let him demean me all day, then he'd had sex with me. Good sex. Intense sex. But no humiliation. No follow-up on his guarantee to make me cum through penetration alone.

No mention of him making me his fuck pig.

CHAPTER 42

I was attaching my seamed stockings to my suspenders when I first realised something was up.

Grady called me again.

"In a minute, honey," I said. "I'm just making myself presentable for you."

He came into the bedroom, holding my mobile. "I think you should take this."

I did up the last suspender, then took my phone.

"Your sister seems worried," he said.

The morning sun shone through the window onto my bare back, as I caught up on Jenny's texts.

Grady watched me.

I saw concern on his face, not control.

"I didn't open them, angel, but I saw the first few words."

I nodded. "It's okay, Grady. No secrets between us. She's asking me what's wrong. Why can't I pick her up?" I looked at the time. "Her flight would've landed a couple of hours ago. She keeps asking about the car." I glanced up to my lover. "She hasn't shown any concern for me."

He came forward and put his arms around me. "You're my concern now... And ol' Grady is gonna take good care of you."

I set my mobile on the bed, then hugged him back. "I'm not sure what to do."

"About your sister?"

I giggled. "No, silly, about underwear... Should I make this another no panty day?"

"Oh, baby, that would be perfect." He hugged me tighter, then kissed my forehead. "You know I love your little clitty on show all day."

I giggled to myself as I presided over his breakfast, knowing he'd no idea of my secret invention hidden underneath my dress.

"I wish I could read your mind, baby," he said, watching me. "I know you're up to something."

I grinned, then nodded.

"What?"

I pointed to the kitchen table. "Sit down. Be patient, Grady. You'll see."

He pulled out a chair, sighed and then sat. He began to whistle.

I twirled as I turned, revelling in the moment my dress rode almost high enough to reveal my clitty. *Almost*, but not quite. I set down his full English breakfast.

"You're not having?" he asked.

The toaster popped. "That's mine there." I grabbed the single slice. "I'm watching my feminine figure for you."

He tucked into his meal.

I sat at the chair immediately to his right, crossing my legs, then adjusting my dress so it showed off so much more flesh.

"Your legs are *so* smooth, angel."

"I've always been pretty naturally hair-free, Grady, but I'll make sure to keep myself totally and utterly while I'm here."

He glanced at me. "While?"

I nodded, knowing I'd too often alluded to a possible intention of not staying permanently.

He chewed on his bacon.

I loved how my bra sat under my dress.

"You said you told your sister you wouldn't be going back."

"Yes," I said.

"Was that true?"

I spread my legs as wide as I could, then held up my dress to reveal my sex.

Grady dropped the sausage from his fork.

I said nothing.

"*That's* what you did when you were out in the garden earlier?" he asked, blinking as if in disbelief.

I smiled. "You like?"

"Yes, baby." He reached out to touch me between my legs.

I swatted his hand away. "No touching, Grady, I don't want you to break it." Around my clit, I was wearing a string of daisies I'd tied together by their stems.

He stared.

"Don't let your food get cold, darling."

Grady tried to eat, but he was so distracted.

"I can always put it away again-"

"Don't you dare," he insisted, then downed his food as fast as he could. "The sight of you like that's driving me crazy."

"Good."

"I didn't think a daisy chain could be so sexy."

I bent one leg at the knee, then stretched it over the knee of the other, keeping my thighs apart. "You mean you doubted I could pull it off?"

"No, angel, no... I mean I just never thought of it."

I touched his elbow. "I'm kidding you... Sir."

He ate even faster. "I desperately want to make love to you, Maxine."

"No, not going to happen."

He growled.

"I don't want you to make love to me, Grady."

He scowled.

"I want you to go about *your* chores today. Your manly, hard-working chores."

"Maxine," he warned, his tone almost scornful.

"Flex those muscles of yours, Grady. Give them a good work-out. Build up a hell of an appetite. Then I'll feed you a feast for dinner." I leaned myself backwards on the chair and pushed my rear forward, hoping just a hint of my hole might become visible underneath my she-scrotum. "Maybe we can shower together after that. Or maybe you'll just want to take me somewhere and give me a good, hard fucking... Treat me like the fuck pig I long to be treated like."

"Maybe not." His eyes were only on his plate.

"What?"

"Maybe not, Maxine."

"But I need it," I said, feeling my heart palpitate.

He shrugged.

"Grady, please. I need to be taken like that. I need to be treated like that. Don't make me beg."

He ate some more.

"Grady-"

"Beg."

What? "You're not really going to make-"

"Beg for it, or you can spend another day on the porch. Naked again, if you like."

I grinned. Oh fuck, this was when I really adored my man. When his mood would change in an instant. When he'd go from caring to cold and heartless in a split-second.

"Beg, slut."

"Fuck pig," I pleaded. "Call me fuck pig."

"Slut."

I wheezed, wanting to slip a hand into my bra to fondle my nipples. "I think it's the only way you'll make me cum without touching her." I yearned for his eyes to take to my clitty again.

His eyes didn't move.

"Look at the daisy chain, sir."

He ignored me.

"Please, I made it for you, sir."

He sliced a sausage in half, then stuffed it into his mouth.

"I'll stay for good, if you make me cum..." I felt heat rise within me as I staked my life on it. "Through penetration alone..." As I put my whole existence in his hands. "I promise you, sir."

"You'll have to do better than that," he said.

I lifted my dress over my head and threw it onto the floor.

His eyes never left his plate.

I stood from the chair, then crawled on all fours onto the table. "Please, sir, I want you to make me your fuck pig. I'm *really* begging you for your cock. I want to feel it violently tear into my hole. It's *your* hole now, after all. She belongs to you. All of me does-"

"Yeah, yeah, slut." He chewed the last of his egg. "I'm nearly finished here, I should go make a start on my day's work since there's fuck all happening here."

I put my varnished fingernails on the edge of his plate. "Finish your food first," I dared snap. "Your fuck pig's not finished talking."

His eyes moved to my mine.

I slid onto my side, letting my soft clit dangle across one thigh.

He glared at her.

"Go do your fucking work, sir, but then promise me you'll come back and gut my anus like the filthy, useless fuck pig you know you've always wanted me to be."

His nostrils flared.

"Yes, sir, that's it... See how inadequate your fuck pig makes you feel when you're not fucking her like the slutty whore you know she's been with *all* those other men before you."

Grady slammed down his knife and fork.

I wasn't fucking done. "I *was* going to give myself to Nick that night you saved me. I honestly was. I made you wait days to fuck me."

He shoved his plate across the table.

"Aw, are you feeling sorry for yourself?" I patted my slit. "You want to rip off my daisy chain?"

He was beginning to sweat.

"You can't," I whispered. "You're forbidden from touching me... Not until you call me fuck pig."

Grady stood up suddenly, sending his chair flying backwards onto the tiled floor.

"Go to work then. I'll *probably* still be here when you get back." I glanced at my mobile on the edge of the table. "Unless I get a better offer."

He grabbed my phone, stuffed it in his pocket and headed into the living room to grab his jacket.

"Maybe you should confiscate my car keys too," I shouted, running my fingers down one stocking.

He hauled open the front door.

"You wouldn't want me driving off while you're slaving away at your manual labour without me."

He slammed the door behind him.

I was almost giddy. I loved this fucking sex-on-legs of a man so much. I knew I'd pay for my rebellious attitude later. "Oh, clitty," I cooed, knowing the sex he'd give me would make it all so worthwhile. "I can't wait to be his fuck pig."

CHAPTER 43

I'd made the cottage spotless for his return, and moved his dinner fresh from the oven onto the table the moment he stepped through the front door.

I could smell his day's toil from his body as we ate in silence.

I nervously bobbed the stiletto of one crossed leg over the other.

He quickly finished his feast, then unbuttoned his shirt.

I was disappointed when he took himself off down the hall to the bathroom before he'd finished undressing. I needed to see his naked body again.

Grady entered the bathroom. Seconds later, he was in the shower.

I tidied the kitchen, irked he hadn't acknowledged me in any way. Never mind indulged my fuck pig prerequisite.

The sun was starting to set.

I wondered would he have to rush off to his mother's or if he'd already been while he was still outside. I knew I daren't ask.

He was whistling.

My clitty stirred.

I walked quietly across the kitchen floor, feeling my stocking tops glide together, then down the hall. I peered into the bathroom.

The shower glass was steamed up.

Nevertheless, I walked confidently into the bathroom, allowing my heels to click loudly on the floor.

He turned around.

I slid the door open.

Grady watched me.

I saw his cock was soft, yet still adorable. I felt for the frilly ends of my dress, taking hold then slowly lifting them up my thighs. I felt my clit and daisy chain come into his view, then tugged the dress higher over my waist and eventually right over my head. I discarded it on the floor.

He said nothing.

I slipped one hand into a cup of my bra and tweaked my nipple. "I'm your fuck pig, sir."

He pressed the palm of his right hand into his thigh, right next to his cock.

I gasped as I hurt myself, then swapped to the other nipple.

He was stiffening.

I gently ran the forefinger of my free hand on my clit.

"You'll break your daisy chain," he said.

"I won't, sir... *You* will... In fact, you'll break more of me than just this chain."

He was rigid.

I bent forward, parted my lips and took him into my mouth as warm water cascaded down his body. Oh God, he tasted incredible. I hungrily sucked all I could of him. This cock truly was amazing. I felt at his balls too, squeezing them and pushing them back and forth, left and right. I wanted them to stay full for as long as possible, emptying only when he'd made me jettison my juices through an anal pounding alone.

Yet I took his shaft to my throat regardless. His behemoth was just so demanding of the deepest depths. He was too big to be toyed with in my mouth alone. I needed to find ways to accommodate this girth, even all the way to my trachea if heavenly possible.

He grunted.

I knew I was doing good, but I had to do better. I concentrated hard on ignoring my reflux, to overcome it if at all possible, and slid him down as if I was literally swallowing him.

"Yes," he croaked. "More." Grady involuntarily flexed his stomach muscles, splashing water on my face.

I flinched.

The head of his cock hit the back of my throat.

I couldn't help coughing, and retreated my mouth to catch my breath.

Grady took hold of my head. "No, you don't get away that easily..." He slid himself back down again. "Fuck pig."

I surrendered my throat to his power. To his might. To his outright authority over me.

"Good girl."

My clit became totally erect within my daisy chain.

Grady hauled me all the way into the shower with him, backing himself against the wall and sending the spray of water onto my back.

I ensured his cock never left my mouth, sucking him more

earnestly even if I couldn't keep up the earlier depth.

"Yeah, you like that, fuck pig? You like cock in your face? You're not bragging about all the men who've had you before now, are you? No, slut, you're taking ol' Grady's cock and you're taking it good."

I nodded my mouth on his rod, as water splashed on my seamed stockings.

He pulled it out and planted his scrotum on my lips. "Lick my balls, whore."

"Yes, sir," I rasped, then took them feverishly in turn into my mouth. I tried to get both in at once, but I couldn't quite manage it.

Grady shoved me back, showering my face in warm water.

I knew my make-up was ruined and I'd look a tragic, whorish mess... Yet I knew that was kind of the point.

"Oh, fuck pig." He slapped his cock hard across my face.

I was shocked by how much it stung-

Until he did it again. And again. He was beating me with his shaft!

I opened my mouth, about to tell him to take it easy-

Grady forced my face back under the stream of water.

It flushed down my throat. I started to cough. I felt like I was going to spew-

He smashed his cock back in my mouth, and vigorously humped at it. "Yes, fuck pig, that's it!"

I was choking. I tried fighting him off.

Grady easily fended me off. "Take it, you sissy slut!"

I gulped down the warm water, feeling it fall to my stomach, and his cock fed down to my throat again.

His balls were practically bolted to my chin, as he laughed. "Good girl, that's it, showing me what a born subordinate you are."

I whimpered under him.

"Don't you dare beg me to stop, fuck pig, don't you fucking dare!"

I could feel my resolve weaken to the point of surrender, and with it my eyes welled up.

Grady pushed me off him by my forehead. "You're crying?"

I shook my head.

He slapped his cock hard off my cheek. Then again on the other side. "Get over here!" he yelled, and grabbed my hair, trailing me into the corner of the shower. My stockings were soaked right through. He stepped over me, then planted his foot on the top of my back, pushing my head down and my ass high. "Yes, fuck pig, you know what your fuck hole's for. No fucking about with you anymore today."

I swallowed, as water flowed down my flesh in both directions, soaking my head, my hole and my poor, little daisy chain.

Grady powered into my asshole.

I put my hand up on the wall to steady myself and channelled the remainder of my self-control back to my throat, this time to resist unleashing a more masculine grunt.

The condom wrapper washed around the water beneath us.

Grady had hold of me by my hips, as he volleyed his throbbing member in and out of me. "Ho, ho, baby, this is an ass pussy to die for!"

I growled, as one of my suspenders snapped.

He smacked my buttocks. "Fuck up, fuck pig! *I'm* in charge here. I'll call you what I want, when I want."

NO!

He rammed his fat cock high up my hole, tearing at my innards.

I rasped my total – joy and – disregard for my health, then looked down and saw daisies clog around the plug hole. My chain had been truly broken now.

Grady grabbed at my hair, pulling and arching my back.

Water washed off my spine to my sides.

"Who's my whore?" he demanded, as another suspender broke.

"Me!"

"You ready to abandon your life as a boy?"

I was hurt he'd even use that word. "I'm a girl!"

"*My* girl, Maxine?"

"Yes, Grady! I'm *your* girl. *Your* whore. *Your* slut. I'm your *fuck pig* forever, sir."

He drilled his dick into my rectum. "I want you to live here. Permanently. I want you to forget your old life."

I involuntarily gritted my teeth.

"Will you do that, fuck pig?" he asked.

My clitty was oozing precum. "If you can make me orgasm here... Yes."

He raised himself up off one knee so he could fuck down into me with renewed force.

I yelped between agony and ecstasy.

"I could give you an orgasm at any fucking minute I choose, angel."

My palm slipped on the wet wall and I heard yet another suspender ping free.

"Ready?" he asked.

I nodded, pulling his fingers with my long locks.

He jammed himself right down into me.

I smacked my forehead off the wall. "Oh fuck, Grady-"

He pulled back, then in. Out, then in. Up, then in. His bloated balls slapped against mine as he fucked me. "Shut up, fuck pig, this is what you want."

"Yes." I placed both palms on the wall, yet my sex was crying out for attention. Just a few strokes would do it.

"No fucking touching yourself!"

"I know, sir, I know. I wouldn't dream of it!"

He snarled as he ploughed into me.

I was grimacing as I felt a familiar – yet unexpected – heat rise inside my body. My clitty was solid as a rock, pointing high and forward. I could feel my face flush red.

Grady pressed one palm on my back.

My thighs started to vibrate.

He raised himself onto both feet.

My knees threatened to buckle under our weight.

Grady pounded my ass pussy.

I yelled out.

"Are you close, princess?"

I felt his words suppress my oncoming orgasm.

"*Are* you?" he demanded.

I fucking had been!

"Fuck pig?"

That was it! "Yes, sir!" I cried, clenching my sphincter on his shaft. "I can almost feel it!"

Grady gripped my sides, taking me hard under the shower.

My asshole felt red raw all around his cock. "Oh my God, yes!" My clitty was sticking up so hard. "Please, sir!" My tiny she-testicles bounced against his bulging balls. "I'm close." I was wheezing. "So close." My body was edging ever closer to the precipice of no return. "Oh fuck." The last of my suspenders snapped.

Grady buried himself to the hilt inside me, leaned right over my back and whispered in my ear in a gravelly voice, "Fuck pig."

My eyes rolled back in my head, my nylon-clad legs almost collapsed under me and I felt an unbelievable tremble unfold in my loins.

"Fuck pig," he said, remaining motionless inside me.

My fingernails dragged down the tiled wall, as my breathing became ever more ragged.

He pulsated against my prostate. "Fuck pig."

"Ugh." I felt the unforeseen rush coming on.

Grady edged his cock backwards.

"Fuck me," I pleaded, the impending emptiness already impeding my approaching orgasm. "Fuck me, sir."

He retreated his cock all the way to the edge of my entrance, leaving just the head inside.

My mouth was all twisted up. My insides in turmoil. My erect clitty ready to shoot with just a single additional stroke. I believed him. I could feel it. I was certain. "Fuck me, Grady! I want to cum! I'm ready!"

Grady pulled me up by my bra.

I anticipated his teeth on my neck as he speared me into my climax.

"Any minute I choose," he said.

My chest rose.

"But not this one." He yanked his cock out from my asshole.

I cried out. "No, Grady! No! No, sir, no!"

CHAPTER 44

My seamed stockings ripped on the stones outside the front door, as Grady dragged me along.

"Come on, fuck pig."

I staggered to my feet, almost keeling over on one heel.

"Kick them off," he barked.

"What? My stilettos?" I looked at the stones. "You can't expect me to walk over these on my bare feet?"

Grady came right up to my face.

I could feel his erection poke my lower abdomen.

"What I expect is my fuck pig to follow every instruction without question." He gestured to Jenny's car. "Or she can fuck off back to her old life."

I slid off my stilettos.

He stepped back, his glorious, muscular body naked, and looked me up and down in my bra, suspender belt and stockings. One stocking had fallen to my calf. The other was above my knee, torn in several places.

"I can't believe you didn't let me cum," I whined.

Grady grabbed me, twisted me around and shoved me forward, bending my back and opening my ass. He pushed his condom-sheathed cock into my entrance again.

"Oh fuck!"

A breeze ruffled leaves in the surrounding trees. Several birds tweeted. Another flew overhead.

I could see the lane which led to his mother's cottage. "Out here?" My soles ached on the stones. "You're going to make me cum out here?"

Grady laughed, then lifted me onto one leg.

I tried to steady myself with my hands as my remaining standing leg shook under his every forceful stroke.

"This isn't about *you*, fuck pig."

I filtered my irrepressible grunt into a squeal.

"This is about me."

My sphincter squelched under his assault.

"This is my property. This cottage. These grounds. And..." He stabbed my rectum. "You."

"Yes, sir... I belong to you."

He reached under my parted legs and found my clitty. "You'll stay here even if she never shoots her juice again."

I was silent but for my groans.

He found my she-balls, then squeezed. "Won't you, fuck pig?"

"I can't take it anymore, sir... I *need* to cum-"

He dropped my second leg back to the ground.

The stones immediately hurt my foot.

Grady pulled out of me, tore off his condom and threw it to the ground. "You'll pick that up later as part of your chores, sissy."

I was breathless. "Yes, sir-"

He hauled me by my hair under the evening sun further away from the cottage.

My feet ached as I tried to tiptoe effeminately over the gravel, past my sister's car. "Oh God, sir, where are you taking me?"

His huge cock smacked off his thighs as he stalked onwards. "Sir?"

He dragged me to the old barn. "Sometimes, fuck pig, not everything is as random and chaotic as it seems." He opened the door, released my hair and gestured for me to go inside. "Sometimes, ol' Grady has everything planned out."

I walked into the cold, dank barn and let my eyes adjust.

"Everything."

I stared at the box of tricks from the bedroom. It was set in the middle of the barn. I knew the contents. Every kinky toy.

Grady closed the door behind him. He sealed it. "You're fucked now, Maxine."

CHAPTER 45

You're fucked now, Maxine.

I took a deep, defiant breath. "No," I stated.

His cock rested between my buttocks, the bulbous head on my lower back, as he clamped his body against mine. "No?" he demanded.

"Not Maxine, sir... Fuck pig-"

He wrenched hold of my clit. "She's so hard, slut."

I tried to gently move myself back and forth in his palm for several seconds. I groaned.

"Stop it, fuck pig."

I instantly ceased moving.

"I want you to lose your erection."

I was still within his hand. "I can't, sir. She's relentless. I don't think you truly understand... I fundamentally *need* to cum."

"You will, slut. I promise. In this room. This evening. You will cum."

I moaned my approval.

"Now lose your erection, fuck pig."

I was so confused. My heart was beating so hard. I was pulsating within his palm.

His cock throbbed over my rump.

"I can't, sir."

"Yes, you can. You can do whatever I tell you to, fuck pig."

I suppressed a sigh. "Sir, I don't want to disappoint you-"

"Then lose it. Go soft. Please your master."

The feel of his huge phallus on my skin only intensified my lust. My she-balls felt on the brink of exploding. If only he'd subtly massage my she-member. "Sir, may I ask just one question?"

He kissed the nape of my neck.

I felt my vein pulse against his hand. "May I?"

"Mm-hm." He traced his lips to my ear lobe.

"*If* I go soft, how am I supposed to cum?"

He stopped kissing me. "*If*? You *will* go soft, fuck pig. Then I will fuck you senseless until you spray your she-spunk all over the ground."

I swallowed. "I don't think I'll last very long, sir. I believe you now. I know it's possible. I know you can make me cum without touching her. I was on the brink in the shower... I know one stroke of your cock inside me and I'll be rock hard again-"

Grady released my she-rod.

She stood firm and naked as I panted, my nipples poking through my bra.

Grady unclasped my suspender belt, then pulled it free from my body. He stepped back, his cock leaving a trail of precum along my lower back to the top of my buttocks. "Fuck pig," he whispered, then walked around me, surveying the size of my clit. "Look how big those girly balls have got."

"They're unsavoury," I admitted.

Grady nodded.

"Sorry, sir."

He stared at my genitals.

I felt my shame only serve to increase the blood flow to my sex. Why was she behaving with almost male-like wanton selfishness? My master demanded she should go down, so why wouldn't she deflate?

He ran the tip of his tongue over his lips.

I imagined him taking her into his mouth again.

"I'm not going to fellate you this evening, fuck pig."

I gulped. "Of course not, sir. Sorry." How the fuck did he read my mind so well?

"Don't look at me," he said. "Look at the box."

I glanced to the box. Just the thoughts of all those terrifying implements inside brought my body out in goosebumps.

"Are you scared?"

"Yes, sir."

"You should be." He pinched hold of the tip of my clit. "You *really* should be." He squeezed her tight.

I placed my hands on my hips, and dug my fingernails into my skin to distract from the pain.

Grady crushed the tiny head of my she-penis.

I squealed out, then pulled away.

He laughed at me. Then he stopped suddenly. "You're still as hard as ever."

I looked at him. "Sir, I'm-"

"Look at the box, bitch, not me!"

I did so, as I felt my second stocking also fall to my calf. "Sorry, Grady... Sir."

He sighed.

"Master."

Grady turned, then lifted the lid off the box. "Let's see," he said.

"Hmmm," he said, as he set the sixth and final dildo on the ground before the box.

I was in awe at the sheer size of it. Each had been bigger than the first, which was easily eight inches, but the final one was horse-sized!

"I know you can take these, angel."

Angel? Was that how he'd manipulate me?

"The question is... Do I really want my fuck pig gaping wide for the next week?" He looked at me, as he ran his fingers down the handle of the horse dildo.

I hoped the question was rhetorical.

"Of course I do," he said.

Anxiety heaved in my chest, thrusting my titties high.

Grady looked back in the box.

I felt the smallest relief at my momentary reprieve.

He lifted out a selection of whips.

I gasped.

"Quiet, fuck pig."

I clamped my mouth shut.

"Don't make me muzzle you," he added, lifting out a particular gag. "Besides, I wouldn't whip you..." Grady pulled out a pair of handcuffs. "Not without restraining you first with these... Or this." He held up a bondage harness.

I was struggling not to fidget, my body's fear reducing my instincts to total intimidation. I could not run – I *would* not run – yet I couldn't quite stand still as my master set out yet more ways of punishing my lithe, innocent body.

"Oh, fuck pig, we could have such fun with this, you sure you want to cum?"

I nodded profusely. "Please, sir. Please. I beg of you. Don't use that on me. I couldn't take another denial."

He threw the ball lock back in the box. "Shame."

I ran my fingers through my long mane of hair as Grady threw out half a dozen packets of condoms. How many times did he think he was he going to tear into my asshole before I'd finally cum? I was still *so* close. Just a few strokes of my-

"This," he said proudly, lifting up the armbinder. "And this." He held aloft the metal anal hook. "They'll make for such a devastating combination." He set them out, then reached into the box again. "Where's the blindfold and gag? They're in here somewhere. I should suffocate all your other senses."

"Suffocate?" I asked, pirouetting over panic.

"Trust me, fuck pig."

I strove to channel my efforts into regulating my breathing.

"You will most certainly learn to when I flog the shit out of you with this," he said gruffly, then lifted out a whip I'd missed days before. "The cat o' nine tails, fuck pig."

My breathing went ragged.

Grady laughed.

I started to back away.

His nostrils flared and his eyes flushed with rage.

I froze my heel in mid-air, then promptly returned it to its previous spot. "Sir, please don't use that on me. I'm not into being hit-"

"How do you know, slut?"

"I..."

"How many men have you let whip you before?"

"None!" I hesitated. "Sir."

Grady's erection was huge as he walked towards me, swishing the brutal instrument through the air. "You're lying, fuck pig."

I felt my bra tighten as my terror grew.

"You know I can read you like a book."

My abdomen shrank, as if in anticipation of the fierce striking after striking I was about to receive.

"I can read your mind, Maxine."

"One," I whispered, my eyes only on the whip.

He ran it over my chest, then my chin, forcing me to tilt my head back. He slipped his tongue between my lips.

I was too frightened to kiss him back.

He swirled my tongue around my mouth, then he pulled out and walked around me, running the nine knotted thongs of the whip across both my buttocks. "This will literally lacerate your skin, fuck pig, did you know that?"

I felt moisture slip down my face. My make-up was a mess from the shower anyway, but still I tried to fight it.

"Can you imagine the pain you'll feel afterwards when I fuck you?"

I shook my head. "I've only experienced gentle play before, sir."

Grady laughed, then threw the cat o' nine tails violently down on the dildos. "There's nothing gentle about me, fuck pig!" He slapped my ass, stinging me wildly.

I screamed, as much through the anticipation of what would follow than the actual impact itself. I jutted out for him to reassuringly rub my skin better.

Grady was already returning to the box.

"Sir, I'll do anything you ask of me."

"I know you will, fuck pig."

I stopped. I wouldn't begrudge his needs with the burden of my own limits. If he wanted to beat me, so be it. I looked at the cat o' nine tails again. "I love you."

He laughed.

I felt so timid and worthless... Yet somehow electric and alive. This man's hold over me was amazing.

"No, my dear fuck pig, I really *do* know you will." He removed something from the box, but hid it behind his back as he turned.

I nodded, reluctantly as I was somewhat confused.

Grady smiled.

I feared that smile almost as much as I revered it.

"You are perfect, Maxine."

"Fuck pig," I whispered.

"Yes, fuck pig, you are perfect." He grasped my clit.

I looked down in shock.

"All soft for Grady..."

I hadn't even noticed her go down.

"Just like I asked."

He brought his hand from around his back.

I'd been so frightened of the implements he'd set out I hadn't even felt my clitty change.

"I'm going to clamp you in chastity," he said, and stuffed my tiny sex into a slightly too big cage.

"What are you doing, Grady?"

He somehow tightened it into place.

"Sir, how am I supposed to cum if she can't get hard?"

He laughed, fastening all parts of my clit, from the base to the middle to the tip, within the confines of the chastity cage.

"Sir, this isn't fair," I whined, as he sealed the cage with a padlock. "You're going to use *all* these implements on me, and I can't even get hard?"

"Should you get hard, fuck pig?"

I watched the fires in his eyes. "Not unless you wish, master."

"Should you get to cum, fuck pig?"

"Not unless you wish, sir."

He seized my jaw, aggressively, then squeezed my mouth until my lips were out of shape. "I already told you I can give you an orgasm at any minute I choose." He playfully jiggled my clamped, lifeless sex up and down. "This is only the beginning, Maxine." He grinned. "Oh, angel, you're in for the most intense, extreme fuck of your life... A true test of endurance." He released my jaw.

I dragged in a deep breath.

"I hope you can survive it, fuck pig, I truly do."

I gulped. "Survive?"

He hauled me forward, shoving me onto all fours.

CHAPTER 46

Survive.

I strutted down the hall of Grady's cottage on a pair of white, six-inch stiletto heels.

Go back inside. Wash your face. Fix your make-up. You look like a fucking disgrace, fuck pig.

I was back to my immaculate best as I walked through the living room to the front door.

Then pick out what you most want to wear for me, but know it'll probably be torn to shreds... Just like you, fuck pig.

I was so proud of my choice, as I left the cottage and walked back towards the barn, ignoring my sister's car outside.

And don't you dare try to tamper with your chastity cage. You're a girl now. You shouldn't be getting erections in the first place.

My she-balls were aching for release, yet I hadn't dared touch the cage or my genitals.

I knocked on the barn door.

"Enter, fuck pig," he barked.

I first set one stiletto inside, then the other.

Grady's cock twitched when he saw me. "*That's* what you chose to wear?" He grinned. "I expected more fear from you, fuck pig."

I gulped as I glanced to all the implements laid out on the ground.

"I'm impressed."

"Thank you, sir." I nervously entwined my hands in front of my groin, then looked down.

"Come to me, Maxine."

I ignored him.

"Do what you're told, fuck pig."

I immediately obeyed him. I knew what my true identity was while we were within the confines of this barn... Of this sexual torture house.

He put his palm out to stop me at an arm's length from him, then he let his eyes wander my body.

"Sir," I whispered, "I love you."

He reached to my hands, running his fingers over the rings I wore, then to my wrists, caressing my bracelets. He looked up to the big gold hooped earrings, then to the choker around my throat. Grady gazed at my naked tits, then smiled as he took in the tight belt around my waist. It was my only attire but for a pair of tanned hold-up stockings and my white heels. "I love no panty day, fuck pig."

"Yes, master."

He gripped me by my buttocks, pulling me tight to him. "How does your asshole feel now?"

I hesitated, knowing all those dildos were lined up to next to each other. "Empty, sir."

Grady licked my lips, but wouldn't kiss me despite my attempts to lure his tongue inside. "Lie down on your back, fuck pig."

I lowered my rear onto the cold ground, then gasped as my bare back felt the same surface.

Grady gripped the chastity cage, shaking my sex from side-to-side. "Does that give you any pleasure?" he demanded.

I shook my head.

He lowered his mouth between my legs and began to lick at my testes.

I groaned.

"Does that bring you any relief, princess?"

"A little," I confessed, forgetting myself.

"We can't have that." Grady retreated his head from my groin. "Fuck pig's aren't supposed to get relief." He ripped open a condom, then slid it over his hard member. "Raise your ass for me, fuck pig."

I did as I was told, relieved in so many ways that he was going to fuck me with his cock and not any of the dildos. Especially not the horse-sized one!

"Let's open up your whore ass."

I pulled my cheeks wide for him.

Grady smiled as he lowered his body on top of mine, positioning his cock at my hole. "You'll only cum when I want you to cum."

I panted my warm breath over his mouth. "Kiss me," I pleaded.

He ignored me.

"If I never want you to cum, you'll *never* get to cum." He started to ever so slowly slide himself into me. "Not even in your sleep."

My clitty stirred in her cage.

Grady leaned my legs back, pinning them under his shoulders. "I wonder how many men have fucked you like this before me."

My sphincter stretched around his shaft. I groaned. "You're so fucking big, master."

"How many?"

I felt his abdomen rub against my caged clitty. "No one's ever fucked me like you, sir."

Grady snarled as he pierced my rear to the hilt.

I gasped, grateful to be his to do with as he pleased.

He propelled himself faster.

I tried in vain to kiss him again.

He deliberately drooled on my face.

I licked up his saliva like the bitch in heat I was. "I want to be yours forever, sir."

"Shut up. You just want to cum."

I tried to rub my caged clitty against his stomach.

Grady laughed. "You really think that'll make you cum, you stupid whore?"

My heels pointed up high in the air, as my anus contracted around his glorious, mammoth cock. "I'm going to let you do this to me every day, Grady."

He spat into my mouth.

I'd normally have been abhorred by such a disgusting act, but with him I only craved more and hungrily sucked it down my throat.

"You just wanna cum and go, fuck pig."

I vehemently shook my head. "I'm *never* leaving you, sir. I promise you."

He stabbed my hole.

I squealed out, dragging my fingernails down his muscular back.

"You're a sycophant, fuck pig."

A what?

"You'll say anything your sissy ass can think of to get your own way."

I desperately clung myself close to him. "I just want to make you happy."

He planted his palm over my entire face, blinding me and muffling my cries. "I should make you sleep in here at night. Change it up. Make it less a barn. And more a sty." He squeezed my face. "A fucking pigsty."

My clit somehow felt alive in her cage.

Grady manipulated his torso so he never touched it as he

pummelled me on the cold ground.

I mumbled under his hand.

"Shut up, slut. You know I can read your mind. I already know the pathetic shit you're gonna say to try to get out of your cage."

I felt my face redden with embarrassment. How did he know me so well?

"I won't let you out of it, fuck pig. You live in it now."

But I needed to cum so fucking bad!

He pulled his palm away, then spat over my face, coating my lips, cheeks and eyes.

I hadn't even captured any in my mouth.

Grady spat on me again.

I felt the life surge to my sex. Yet she couldn't grow! She was so very stimulated yet so very stifled. "Grady?" I shrieked in agony. "Will you *ever* let me cum?"

He snarled. "At the very moment I choose."

I looked down at my caged clitty bouncing beneath him. "It's impossible."

He laughed, slamming himself harder into me.

"Spit on me," I begged. "Spit on me like I'm nothing."

"You are nothing."

"Like I'm worthless-"

Grady spat on my eyes again.

I could feel my mascara run.

"Fuck pig," he said, as if seething. He pulled suddenly out of me.

I cried out, the sounds of my terror echoing off the four walls of the barn.

He pumped his cock in his fist. "I shouldn't even bother wearing protection with you."

I felt true fear grip me all over, yet still my sex throbbed impossibly. "I've never been bare-backed... Never."

"How many men?" he demanded.

"What, sir?"

"How many men have fucked you before me, fuck pig?"

I was shocked at his bluntness.

"I order you to tell me right now."

I had to do a quick count in my head.

"Hurry up."

I was still counting.

Grady sneered. "*That* many, slut?"

I was making sure I made no mistakes. He'd know if I did. I took out a few of the guys I'd only sucked and came close to my true, final number.

"Tell me now, fuck pig."

"Seventeen," I said, gasping. "Seventeen men have fucked my ass before you, sir.

"Turn around."

"I'm sorry, I-"

"Get on all fours."

I felt him enter me again. "Fuck!" It felt like he was still sheathed. Yet my anus was so sore from all the fucking I couldn't be certain.

He shoved my head to one side and down onto the cold ground. "It's still on, you stupid, scared whore."

"I *would* do it for you," I said, grimacing through the pain. "I'd sleep in here if you told me to. I'll do anything you tell me to, sir. I'm never leaving you."

He grabbed hold of my choker in one hand, as he fucked me, and my belt in the other.

I heard myself grunting under his onslaught.

"Look at all those implements," he said. "I can use any of them on you, any time I choose. Or I can use none of them. Deprive you of them. Make you wish for them." His cock ripped at my rear. "But know I know you better than you know yourself, fuck pig."

"I know, sir!"

"You really think you can't cum in your chastity cage?"

I shook my head.

"You will, fuck pig. I promise you. The moment I want you to orgasm, you will orgasm. And you'll leave such a dirty, slutty mess on the ground... I may even make you lick it all up."

Oh my God! "Yes, sir!" I felt a wave of fever envelope my entire body. "This can't be possible!"

Grady snarled as he slammed into my hole. "I haven't told you to cum yet, slut."

My clitty flopped back and forth, matching the motion of his huge member inside me. "I'm so close, sir. Honestly, I think I'll only last a matter of seconds after you unlock me-"

Grady strangled me with my choker. "I won't be unlocking you, you stupid whore cunt!"

I was choking.

He was relentless.

I couldn't speak.

He funnelled faster into me.

Oh my God, was this how he'd do it? I'd only read about it before.

Grady dragged my throat first one direction, then roughly in another.

I feared I'd blackout.

He tightened his grip.

I feared I'd be murdered.

He smashed into my asshole.

I feared I'd never fucking cum.

Grady shoved my head so violently forward it broke my choker.

I wheezed, desperate for breath.

He broke off my belt, then wrapped it around my throat, pulling either side of it so tight my air supply was completely cut off.

My fingernails dragged on the dank ground.

"No, fuck pig, you're wrong."

Wrong? I was gagging. Wrong about what?

"This isn't how I'll make you cum."

My eyes were bulging.

"This is merely how I'll terrify you."

I tried to break free from him to no avail.

"Show you how dangerous I am."

I flung my hands through mid-air.

"And how vulnerable you are."

My vision was distorting.

"If I want to fuck you to death out here in the middle of nowhere, fuck pig, then that's exactly what I'm gonna do."

I struggled pathetically to free myself from him.

"I could murder you in a heartbeat, fuck pig."

I even attempted to wriggle my hole away from his hard on.

"Stop it!" he barked. "Listen to your master."

I froze. I was choking. I was close to passing out. I'd just had my life threatened. And yet still I diligently obeyed him.

Grady cackled, then let go of the belt.

I coughed and spluttered.

He grabbed hold of my arms, pulling them behind my back. "You may cum, fuck pig."

I dragged air into my lungs. "What?"

"I said you can fucking cum now!" he yelled, and assaulted my anus with every inch of his unassailable erection.

I was flapping.

"Are you stupid, fuck pig? I said... YOU MAY FUCKING CUM!!!!!"

I felt the most ferocious penetration in my rectum. Stars spun in front of my eyes. I was lifted to existence on some sort of astral plane. My arms were stretched out wide.

Grady held me under them.

I surrendered to every sensation and emotion in my body and mind.

He speared into me.

I was crying out, grunting, squealing and unleashing tears of intensity down my cheeks.

Grady refused to relent.

My clitty was engulfed in my cage.

His body ransacked mine.

I felt a rush in my loins,

He squeezed under my arms.

The rush ran all the way to my crotch. To my softness. To my caged sex.

"Cum, fuck pig."

I ejaculated in the most unbelievable of fashions. I threw my head back and saw the roof of the barn, my prison of lust. My eyes were bulging through pleasure. Wonderful, unbelievable pleasure which every instinct of my anatomy told me was impossible. Yet, it was happening. I was in the throws of an incredible, caged climax, as my lover's cock thrust and throbbed in my rear. I let my eyes fall under my eyelids, as my orgasmic shrieks shook the very structure of the building.

Grady came to a standstill deep inside my anal palace.

I emptied yet more she-sperm from my flaccid clit.

He held me up.

I could feel the cum run down my legs into my tanned stockings.

"Good girl," he said, half-sounding condescending, half-sounding like he was giving an appraisal. "Good, good girl."

I could barely breathe. "Grady-"

"I told you it was possible, angel."

I felt as if I was high.

"I promised you you'd cum on my command."

I nodded, unable to speak.

Grady helped me stand up on my stilettos, then he gently turned me around to face him.

I dared open my eyes, then looked down. My broken choker lay on the ground. My belt was loose, hanging down my chest over my tiny titties. My caged clit was saturated in my juices. And my jewellery-clad fingers still couldn't touch my sex.

"Was that good?" he asked.

I breathed. "Sir, that was amazing."

Grady shushed me. "We can stop the sir, master and fuck pig charade now, Maxine."

"Because I came?"

He nodded.

"But you didn't, Grady."

He was already peeling off his condom. He tossed it aside.

I knew I'd be lifting that one up later as well when I did my chores.

He stooped down.

I couldn't believe it. My Grady was actually going to lift it for me!

Except he didn't. He studied my caged sex. "Beautiful," he remarked, then threw his mouth over it, licking the device and sucking up my spent she-sperm.

I groaned through frustration as much as pleasure. His warm breath on my sex was joyous, but his tongue barely made physical contact.

Grady diligently cleaned my cage, swallowing down my juices. "You taste amazing, Maxine."

"Thank you."

"But I need more." He got up off his knee, grinned at me, then went to the box. "Where is it?" He fished inside for several seconds. "Got it." He held aloft a key.

"You're going to release me?" I asked.

"Yes, princess." He came back to me and unlocked my chastity cage, letting it fall away to the cold ground.

"Grady, I'll wear that for you everyday if you want me-"

He sucked my tiny, soft sex into his mouth, easily taking it all.

I almost lost my balance on my stilettos. "Oh my God, Grady, the way you eat my clitty is unbelievable."

He felt at my she-testes, as if he was checking they were properly drained.

I was a little embarrassed at how small they were again. Although I took sensual comfort in how feminine they felt within his magical touch. I knew he'd be satisfied – if not happy – at how he'd literally fucked them dry.

Grady tried to fellate me faster.

My erection wouldn't rise.

He swirled his tongue all around her.

"You're so good to me, Grady. Cleaning me! At this rate, I won't even need a shower."

He hungrily ate at my clitty.

I saw my she-stains on the ground. Two big puddles and several little ones. I wondered if I should volunteer to go down and lick the ground clean.

He planted his lips at the base of my sex.

I ran my fingers through his hair. This was just too damned good to stop him now!

Grady licked my little length to the tip, then released her. "You're clean now, princess. Just as you should be." He stood, holding his huge cock in his hand. "But you are right about one thing... I didn't get off."

I felt such a disappointment in his eyes.

"No, no, no, Maxine, don't feel bad. You did all I asked of you. I commanded you to cum, and you did. Without *any* stimulation to your tiny clitty. All locked up in chastity and with my cock in your ass, you came bucket loads."

My face flushed red.

He took hold of my sex in his other hand, massaging her gently. "She's so cute when she's this small."

My knees were trembling. My ankles too. I wasn't confident I could stand for much longer in my high-heels.

"What are the chances of you getting hard again?" he asked.

"Quickly?"

I bit my lower lip. "I'm sorry, Grady, I've always been girly in that department... She'll stay small and soft for ages."

He grinned. "Music to my ears, angel." He slapped his big cock over my tiny clit. "Music to ol' Grady's fucking ears." He started to wank both our sexes in his palm, his blatantly superior over mine.

I was still moist from his saliva.

He used it to lubricate his shaft, then he leaned forward and kissed me.

I was putty in his hands.

"How'd I compare to the other seventeen lucky bastards who've fucked you?" he asked, aggressively pummelling cock and she-cock in hand.

"Like a king compares to paupers," I replied, without hesitation.

He grinned, sweat glistening on his glorious body.

"No one ever has or ever will fuck me like you do. I don't want anyone else to ever fuck me, Grady. I'm yours."

He snarled. "You're just saying that."

I shook my head vigorously. "No, Grady, I've came. This is my head and my heart speaking. I want to stay here with you-"

He shushed me. "Talk dirty to me, angel. Talk like a slut. Tell me about those other guys. I want to cum."

I put my forefinger against my mouth and bit into it in as innocent and girly a manner as I could muster. "Really?"

He nodded profusely.

"You want to hear about the different places I've been fucked like a slut?"

"Yes... The more outlandish the better."

I took a deep breath as his massive member crushed my clitty. "I lost my virginity in the grounds of a church. The guy was the minister's son. He wouldn't leave me alone for weeks. It started with me giving him hand-jobs in the back row, where no one could see. Then he started to take me off to a private bible study where he'd make me suck his cock. I did so much sucking that summer. We almost got caught by his father a couple of times. I was terrified. He acted like he wasn't. He was quite used to getting his own way... Taking charge of me."

Grady grunted as he steadfastly jerked our entwined sexes.

"I told him I didn't want to have sex, probably a hundred times or more. One day he took me for a walk. I didn't even realise how secluded the area was until he stopped me in a certain spot. He kissed me, made me play with him as usual, and something about the glorious sunshine just made me drop my defences. I didn't put up a fight when he pulled down my pants. He only played with my clitty a little."

Grady was going crazy, pumping his penis.

My own sex fell free from his palm.

Grady ignored her.

"He said he wanted to fuck me, and started to put on a condom. I made a pathetic excuse about us needing to go back, but he wouldn't hear of it. He just bent me over a big rock and stuck his cock inside me. It hurt. It really did. I didn't enjoy it as much as I should've. He wasn't experienced. He barely knew what he was doing. Well, he knew how to please himself. I just kind of hung onto the rock and let him fuck my ass till he was done with it-"

Grady erupted his spunk, showering my spent clitty and stockings.

I stood smiling, loving his warmth on my skin again.

"Fuck, fuck, fuck!" he cried.

"I *will* have to shower, after all."

Grady wiped the last of his load up and down my she-cock, then slapped his cock off her.

"Aw, Grady, one story down, one orgasm in hand... And another sixteen stories to go."

"Keep them for me," he said, his voice hoarse.

"Okay," I whispered, and began to lovingly rub his sperm into my skin. "I hope you'll like them."

He nodded, then turned to the barn door. "Put everything back in the box. Pick up and dispose of the used condoms. You know the drill when it comes to your chores, angel."

"I do, of course." I was smiling, delighted to be expected to wait on him hand and foot.

"And I'll see you inside for my supper."

CHAPTER 47

I finished reapplying my make-up in the bedroom as Grady ate his supper in the other room. I was naked, and for some reason I didn't feel like wearing clothes again. It was so late in the evening, I figured there was little point.

I slipped into a sexy pair of red heels, nothing else, and headed down the hall to spend time with my man.

His eyes immediately took to my clit. "I fucking love no panty day, Maxine."

I decided to waste little time, and snuggled up next to him on the sofa, wrapping my arms and legs around him.

He kissed my forehead.

"I do love you, Grady," I said.

He grinned. "I'm not kidding, Maxine, yours is probably the most perfect ass pussy I've ever fucked."

I smiled.

"I don't want you to go."

I was silent.

"Tell me you'll stay."

I took a deep breath.

"For real," he added.

I thought of the selfish texts from Jenny. My sister had made it abundantly clear how little I meant to her in reality. I didn't want to go back to her and that life. In actual fact, I'd already binned my mobile when I got back from the barn and laid the car keys out on the kitchen table for him to find.

"I want to hear the stories about all seventeen of those other men, after all."

I giggled, and jokingly slapped his chest.

"So, what d'you say, angel? Will you stay?"

I kissed his lips and stroked his hair and his face. "Don't you remember I already made you a promise, Grady?"

His eyes narrowed.

I crossed my smooth legs over his, and looked down at my beautiful red shoes. "I said if you could make me cum through penetration alone, I'd stay with you."

"Uh-huh."

"Grady, I meant it."

"You'll stay, Maxine?"

I nodded.

"Permanently?"

I pointed to the kitchen. "The keys to my sister's car are on the table. I want you to park the pink fuck mobile in the barn, then hide the keys somewhere I'll never find them." I meant his mother's place, but I still dared not speak of her.

"Why, precisely?" he asked.

I rested my palm on the outline of his fat cock through his boxers. "I won't be needing it for a long time. Maybe never."

He growled. "Explain, Maxine."

I licked his lips. "I'm staying, Grady. Permanently, if you'll have me. I'll take care of you like a traditional wife would a husband. I'll do all my chores. I'll make meals for you and for..." I couldn't say it, so I nodded up in the direction of his mother's cottage. "I'll see to all your sexual needs and fantasies. I'll be your lover, your confidante and, perhaps especially, your filthy, fucking fuck pig."

He went to speak-

I grabbed his wrist. "Okay, maybe I couldn't be fuck pig everyday..."

He raised one eyebrow.

"But if you insist I do become your fuck pig everyday, I hope you know my feelings for you well enough now that I'll do anything you want. Anything at all. If it makes you happy, Grady, I'll do it."

Grady smiled. "Honestly, Maxine?"

"Yes, Grady, honestly. I want to spend my life with you now."

He punched the air. "I most certainly will have you!"

I fell into a passionate kiss him, all while holding his bulge.

Grady kissed me so wonderfully, straying his hands to my ass. "Fuck pig on special occasions," he insisted.

"Special occasions, Grady? What like Christmas, Valentine's and birthdays?"

He laughed. "I was thinking more lazy Sundays."

I giggled. "You're incorrigible, but I love it! Yes, once a week sounds good to me-"

"I'll still expect daily blow-jobs, angel."

I squeezed his cock. "Grady, you'll be getting *more* than blow-jobs everyday. I want our sex life every single day. If I've to go a day without you inside me, making love to me or fucking me, I'll go crazy!"

He cuddled me closer. "I love you too, Maxine."

"Really?" I asked, my voice more effeminate than ever.

"Yeah, you're perfect. I'll take care of you too. I'll protect you. You'll only ever have one person in this world you have to fear."

I felt my body engulfed by that all familiar terror he so easily instigated in me. "Who?"

"Me."

I gulped. "Okay... Sir."

He grinned. "You can mention my mother now."

I hesitated, confusion rife in my mind.

"I mean it," he said, and kissed me deeply again. "I tell you what, angel, why don't you go put on your most sophisticated dress."

I gestured to my body. "Why, Grady, don't you appreciate me draped naked over you?"

"Of course. But I'm about to make this official between us." His cock pulsated through his boxers into my palm. "I'm taking you to meet her."

I stared into the whites of his eyes, fearing a trap. "Who?"

He aimed his thumb behind him, towards his mother's cottage. "Say it, Maxine."

I couldn't. He'd taught me so well.

"Go ahead, Maxine, say it. I promise you it's okay now."

I was nodding ever so slightly, terrified of saying the wrong thing. "You... You want me to meet your mother, Grady?"

"Yes, angel, I truly do." He caressed my nipples on my flat chest. "I want to introduce you to her tonight, as my girlfriend."

THE END

9 798569 578672